5/98

T

ISLAND BOUND

B E T T Y
L E V I N

ISLAND
BOUND

Greenwillow Books, New York

Library of Congress Cataloging-in-Publication Data
Levin, Betty.
Island bound / by Betty Levin.
        p.   cm.
Summary: While trying to prove he can survive
on an island off the coast of Maine, Chris Fossett
meets Joellen Roth, who has come to the island
with her father to work on a puffin research
project, and the two become caught up in a mystery
surrounding the island's 150-year-old ghost.
ISBN 0-688-15217-1
[1. Mystery and detective stories.
2. Maine—Fiction.   3. Islands—Fiction.
4. Ireland—Emigration and immigration—Fiction.]
I. Title.
PZ7.L5759Is   1997
[Fic]—dc21
96-45411   CIP   AC

FOR
ELLEN AND ROY

1

Chris couldn't believe it. Here he was, just sprung from school and ready to cut loose, and instead he was bound for Fowlers Island, where his best friends would leave him to spend his only full week of freedom in total isolation. He had better things to do before starting his summer job at the Harbor View Inn. He ought to have his head examined.

He glanced back at Ledgeport. If someone was going to stop them and ask where they thought they were going, it had to be now. But everyone on the waterfront was used to the three boys taking off like this on a Sunday. No one took any notice of them.

The small workboat wasn't designed for speed, but the boys could make it cover a lot of water. Of course they had to go slow and easy until they were clear of the harbor. But as soon as they headed into Grace Narrows, nothing but the old one-lunger engine could hold them back. Letting go like that usually made Chris feel good. But not today.

It had started last fall with the kind of boasting that so easily sets a trap. Even with three town boys against one from away, Chris and Andy and Eric had felt pressed to challenge Gary. And all because Gary had returned to his summer home bragging about the two nights he had spent alone on Brimstone Island.

Anyone could do that, the town boys had retorted. They didn't need survival training either. Look at all the times Chris stayed out on one of the islands with his father tending sheep. Anyway, Brimstone was small. No one had ever lived on it in bygone days, so you wouldn't meet up with old ghosts and that.

Ghosts? They believed in ghosts? Gary had laughed and laughed.

So one of them had mentioned the light that used to be seen on Fowlers Island on certain moonlit nights. Not the signal from the lighthouse that marked the treacherous ledges of the outer islands, but a low, faint flicker like a candle flame. Most of the old-timers hereabouts had glimpsed it at least once. Or else they knew someone who had. Anyway, they believed it, even if they didn't all agree on what caused it or what it signified. Try staying way out on *that* island.

Gary had shrugged. He figured it was a lot easier spending a couple of nights on a big island where people used to live than on a wild, uninhabited island where you could hear the sea all around you no matter where you unrolled your sleeping bag. Besides, if a storm came up, there was always that lighthouse for shelter.

The lighthouse was out of bounds, the town boys replied. Anyway, its downstairs room was usually full of dead birds and bird crap. And maybe something else.

Gary had laughed again. None of that bothered him any. If one of the town boys went out there alone, he would, too. After all, he had made it through survival camp and passed his solo island experience. He knew about marking eggs in a nest to find out which were newly laid. He knew how to grind up burdock roots and which plants were edible raw.

He didn't think he'd have any trouble getting permission from his folks to spend a few days on an island with a lighthouse. He assumed there would be a well. A gallon of water would be enough for a day or two, but not if a person stayed much longer. And they'd have to agree to certain rules, like no food handouts from outsiders and no raiding lobster traps, and only one box of matches. He'd go a day longer than any one of them on that island. No sweat.

Andy and Eric and Chris had each planned to be the one to outsurvive Gary until it became clear that no one's family would put up with any such nonsense.

Then at New Year's Chris's parents had won the prize of a lifetime. The New England Association of Sheep Breeders had awarded them a three-week sheep tour in New Zealand. They put off the trip until early June, when the home farm chores were least demanding.

Grandad moved in with Chris, who made sure that things were going smoothly before proposing to take the week off.

On Fowlers Island? Grandad didn't like that idea, not one bit.

Chris hadn't actually lied to convince him, but he did have to point out that it wasn't all that different from his being out there with Dad when they sheared the island sheep. Nor did Chris mention not bringing food. And he had to promise that his friends would check up on him and report back to Grandad.

Since Gary hadn't yet arrived for the summer, the town boys just assumed that he would agree to this. To be fair, everything would have to be the same for Gary, and Chris would provide him with a map or description of the island.

"Don't forget," Andy remarked as he cut the engine and coasted up to a rocky outcrop below the beach, "even if someone shows up, you keep away from them. No help. Unless," he added, "you're in trouble."

"I won't be," Chris said, tossing the rope onto high ground. He shrugged his backpack up his shoulder, stepped out on rockweed, and sank to his ankles in the frigid water. Andy and Eric laughed. Chris laughed, too, to keep from yelping. Hoisting his water jug and sleeping bag, he splashed shoreward.

The one-lunger revved up, making its usual racket. Chris turned to watch them go. Eric shouted something that must have been pretty funny because both boys doubled over laughing. The boat rocked as it backed off.

Chris could only grin. He wouldn't let them see how he felt, even though it had nothing to do with fear or being spooked. It was more like being shot into space. And it seemed connected to a feeling he had brought with him from the mainland. Grandad's misgivings? But Chris knew this island too well to let an old man's superstitions bug him. He had outgrown all the family lore that formed the bedrock of Grandad's convictions.

Chris's parents used to try to stop Grandad from filling Chris's head full of rubbish about ghost girls and island jinxes and strange, flickering lights. Once when they were

4

out on Spars Island visiting Grandad and he had mentioned a sighting, Mom and Dad had tried to kid him out of it by asking if he thought it was a UFO. Grandad didn't even know what that meant. So they got serious and told him it could be like that smuggling case a few years back. Maybe someone was bringing stuff ashore, even stashing it in the lighthouse and signaling for it to be picked up.

"Maybe," Grandad had agreed.

Mom and Dad had gone out then. They hadn't heard Grandad murmur under his breath, "Or maybe not." They hadn't seen him fix Chris with a hard look, not defiant exactly but purposeful. Let them believe whatever they want, that look told Chris.

Of course that had happened way back when Chris was a believer, too.

2

Joellen lugged one of her father's bags of gear down the ramp. It bumped from tread to tread like a stubborn child holding back.

"Hey, Josie, no!" Dad called up from the cockpit. "That should be carried. Abbie can give you a hand with it."

Joellen stopped mid-ramp and waited. Nothing in the world would make her ask Abbie for help. Her father picked up a carton of canned food and disappeared inside the cabin. He and Mom used to stow the supplies together. Now Dad did it all. Abbie was still learning where things went and seemed unsure of herself, especially when she knew she was being watched. Joellen kind of guessed that if she wanted to, she could make Abbie extremely uncomfortable.

Getting ready to go on one of Dad's bird projects used to be fun. But this year he was anxious and tense. He had already been out on Fowlers Island in March to set things up. Now he was about to find out whether all his planning and work, which had begun five years ago with Mom and had continued up until last year, had succeeded.

Joellen had objected as soon as she had learned that Abbie would be with them the whole time. This was supposed to be vacation time with Dad.

"You know Abbie's living with me now," Dad had said.

"I know she's your ex-student assistant," Joellen had replied evasively.

Dad had sighed. "That, too." He had looked as if he were about to say something more, then thought better of it. "Please, Josie, please try," he had pleaded.

She had snapped, "Don't call me that. I'm too old for Josie. I'm Joellen."

But of course he forgot, especially when he was preoccupied, like now.

Once they were under way and beating out toward open water, Joellen almost forgot, too. She was at *Dovekie*'s helm, alone in the cockpit. Abbie had removed herself from the area of hostility and was seated on the foredeck, her back to the mast. Whenever Joellen had to bring the boat about, Abbie leaned out of the way of the jib as if Joellen were aiming it at her. But *Dovekie* was rigged for single-handing, and there was plenty of clearance up forward. Abbie wasn't likely to be slapped by the shifting sail.

Dad called up from below, where he was sorting papers. "Okay?"

Joellen nodded. They were coming up to the black can, the last channel buoy. In a moment she would have to bring *Dovekie* about again. If Dad had set a course through Grace Narrows, they would have been tacking even more often.

7

Dad climbed partway up to glance at their position. "When we clear Spectacle," he said, "you can head off about ten degrees."

"Black guillemots," Abbie called from up forward. "A few."

"We'll probably find some nesting in our rookery," Dad answered.

"Ten degrees won't clear Shag Ledges," Joellen declared. She knew she was showing off her local knowledge. She knew she was competing with Abbie for Dad's attention.

It worked, too. Dad told her that the tide would be running strong by now. It should lift them clear. "But keep an eye out," he said. "There're plenty of lobster traps to go by, and you can see forever."

Joellen nodded again, satisfied because Dad had shown that he trusted her sailing. Anyway, it was perfect weather for her first time out this season. *Dovekie* seemed alive as she mounted each sea swell and plunged down every trough. Sometimes she seemed to hesitate, poised on a summit as if relishing the prospect of the next drop. Then with something like a shudder of joy she would slide down, Joellen keeping her bow at a slant and guiding her toward another climb.

The farther out they went, the steeper grew the swells. They began to break against the hull. The spray was icy. Every spring it came as a shock to Joellen, who had to learn anew how slowly the sea warmed up from winter.

As they passed the string of islets called the Porcupines, she waved to a man hauling lobster traps onto a boat that bucked and swung in spite of its little staysail. He was dressed for the cold water in yellow rubber overalls and black boots. She wouldn't have minded ducking below to change out of her drenched clothes and put on her foul-weather things, but she was afraid that if she gave up the helm, even for a minute, Abbie might take over.

Joellen stared up at Abbie. How come she wasn't freezing to death up there? Dad, his back to the companionway, was leaning over some charts. He didn't even notice all the spray.

Abbie gave in first, *Dovekie*'s pitching too much for her. Clutching the stays, she turned and crawled until she could swivel and drop into the cockpit and on down the companionway. The next moment Dad had her wrapped in a towel and was rubbing her hard. And kissing her.

Joellen had to hold the tiller in both hands now to keep her course steady. She waited for Dad to catch sight of her, cold and wet, struggling at the helm. But he was busy getting Abbie warm and rolling up his charts before her beautiful long hair dripped on them.

Had Mom suspected that Abbie would be with Dad? Was that why Mom had warned Joellen not to expect things to be the same? All Joellen had been able to think about was sailing with Dad and exploring his bird islands. Of course it wouldn't be the same without Mom. All this last year had been different. But it had never occurred to Joellen that Dad would bring Abbie along on their first time out together. Probably that was why Mom had given Joellen the special notebook that was a journal for writing down her experiences and keeping in touch with her feelings.

Joellen was surprised to see a small open boat slamming from wave to wave as it approached. It was a long way out to sea here, and the boat rode low in the water when it wasn't crashing through the frothy crests. Because *Dovekie* was under sail, she had the right-of-way. So Joellen kept her course. But the small boat kept right on, as if heading for *Dovekie*'s bow.

Bracing herself, Joellen stood up to see better. Two guys,

one at the helm, one bailing. Were they in trouble? She was about to call Dad when she realized they were laughing, both of them having a high old time. And they knew what they were up to, trying to force *Dovekie* off her course.

Some of the townies around Ledgeport found ways to show their contempt for summer people, even though they made a living off them. Probably these boys didn't realize that Dad wasn't like the rich yachtsmen who came and went along the coast. True, *Dovekie* was a sailing vessel, a sloop, but she was Dad's workboat. He always relied on sail power whenever an engine would disturb the birds he studied.

If this was a game of blink, then Joellen wasn't about to give in. Steady as she goes, she told herself. She glanced down at the compass and then fixed her gaze on the sails. Clenching her teeth, she willed herself not to look at the oncoming boat.

She heard its engine roar as it veered off and then swung back, shipping water when a wave hit broadside. The boys hooted and swore until even Joellen's father heard and poked his head up over the cabin deck.

"You kids alone out here?" he called down to them. "That's not a very seaworthy boat."

"Heading back," one boy responded.

"We're cool," the other called with a confident grin. "Finest kind."

Dad returned to the cabin. The boys stared at Joellen. She stared back.

"I guess you think you've got nerves of steel," remarked the boy at the helm.

Unable to think of a good reply, she didn't say anything.

"Next time," the boy went on, "don't be a jerk. You've got more to lose than we do."

"Not if you get tossed overboard," she retorted. But the moment she spoke, her teeth began to chatter so hard that she couldn't get the words out properly.

"What?" called the boys. "What?"

She didn't try to make herself heard. Anyway, the distance between *Dovekie* and the small boat was widening. Looking ahead, Joellen could see the lighthouse on the horizon now. Fowlers Island stood up from the water, the wooded brow to the west so dark a green it was nearly black. She pulled in the mainsheet a bit and headed a few degrees closer to the wind. Soon the rocky cliff appeared, seamed in white where the sea broke all around.

The thrill of arrival hit Joellen as it always did after hours under way. Even though she ached with cold, she was glad she had remained at the helm. She had been flying across the bay. As if in welcome, the sky seethed with birds, their shrill calls drowning out the sound of waves against *Dovekie*'s hull and something Dad was trying to say to her from down below.

Now all Joellen could think of was hot cocoa or soup. Nodding, she reached out toward him.

But instead of handing her a steaming mug, he hoisted himself up beside her and took the tiller from her stiff grasp.

She shouldn't have been surprised. The approach to Fowlers was tricky, especially under sail in a stiff breeze. Dad would want to pick up the mooring line without resorting to the engine.

In the cabin Abbie tried to help her out of her wet things. Joellen shrugged her off. But when Abbie proffered hot soup, Joellen had no choice but to accept it with a grudging thank-you. She sat with the mug wrapped in her hands. As the boat rolled, she could tell that *Dovekie* had turned in around the point. She heard the mainsail drop. Dad must be sailing on the jib now. His feet pounded overhead. She guessed that he had forgotten to free up the boat hook. There. Now the jib whipped back and forth while Dad secured *Dovekie* to the island mooring.

Joellen raised the mug to her lips, and warmth slid down inside her.

3

A whole week. Whose idea was that? Chris couldn't remember. They had all three been set on raising the stakes, on proving that it didn't take survival training your parents paid through the nose for to manage a few days and nights alone on a Maine island. So they had just said whatever came into their heads.

Chris clambered on and over the stony foreshore until he reached exposed roots growing out of rock fissures. Here a few wind-stunted spruce trees provided momentary shelter. Wedging his sleeping bag against one twisted trunk, he leaned his nearly empty knapsack, the coiled rope, and the water jug against this makeshift shelf and considered where he should set up camp. Out of the wind, of course, which was out of the southwest now. But that could change. Close enough to the shore to allow a good fire without danger to the woods.

The few times he and his father had spent a night here they had chosen the lighthouse end of the island. The old house foundation walls and partial cellar hole offered some protection from the wind when they weren't being used as a kind of sheep pen. Dad kept a couple of rolls of stock fence in under the alder trees near the well so that the animals could be confined there for shearing or dosing.

Dad ignored Grandad's distrust of the lighthouse. As far as Dad could tell, the only jinx he knew of was the very real invasion by scientists demanding that end of the island for their puffin project.

Chris hauled his things up to the edge of the woods and found almost at once a narrow sheep path that followed the shoreline. The trouble was that he had to stoop and sometimes crawl to avoid the low branches the sheep could easily walk under. He struggled on for a while and then turned back. He figured it was best to set up camp on this side of Folly Point. Orcutt Cove was a good spot. There would be plenty of mussels to gather at low tide and clams to dig.

What else could he eat? Eggs for sure. But it was too early in the season for beach peas or raspberries, and any strawberries that escaped the birds and sheep were always so tiny that they were little more than a taste and a red smear on the fingers. Lobsters didn't walk up to you and ask to be steamed over an open fire. Feeding crabs might be caught when the tide went out. Chris would be sure to check the falling tide. No other food came to mind just now, although once Dad had had to shoot a lamb that had fallen or jumped down onto a narrow ledge below the cliff at Dread Mans Cove.

The ewe's bawling had drawn Chris and his father to the

spot. But they had no way to rescue the lamb, which kept trying to scramble back onto the overhanging shelf of the cliff. It would eventually fall to the treacherous rocks below or else remain there until it starved. Dad, who always brought a rifle along in case he came upon injured sheep, had sent Chris back to the boat for it. Then, before shooting the lamb, Dad and Chris had cornered the ewe and grabbed her while she was still intent on her baby. Dad had flipped her over to check her udder and had milked her to relieve the pressure before letting her go.

Dad had said that you could butcher and eat a lamb that had to be sacrificed like that, but of course there was no way to retrieve the stranded carcass.

Later, on their way home, they had taken the boat around by Dread Mans Cove, where crows and gulls fought over what remained of the lamb. Above, close to the cliff edge, the ewe still kept watch. Dad had said that in a while hunger would drive her away.

Chris had never eaten one of those island sheep on the spot, although once he had helped Dad butcher a deer on one of the other sheep islands. There had been a big row over it, too. A schooner had cruised by just as Chris's dad had taken aim. The schooner's passengers had yelled up a storm over the killing. Chris's dad had shouted back that he had to clear out deer because of a parasite they carried that was deadly to sheep. The people just kept shouting that the deer had as much right to live there as the sheep did. Dad got so annoyed that he had strung up the deer in plain sight of the schooner and given Chris his first lesson in dressing a fresh carcass.

Well, there would be no roast sheep or venison this week. No bread or crackers or candy or cereal. Chris stopped for a swallow of water, which reminded him that he should check out the old well before dark. When he glanced at his watch, he was surprised to see that it was already getting late. The long days of spring were deceptive. If he were at home or at Andy's or Eric's, things would be stirring in the kitchen by now. He imagined himself unwrapping a frozen pizza to stick in the microwave.

4

Dovekie swung on the mooring, the dinghy snubbed up close, loaded and ready for the short but tricky landing. But Joellen's father took no chances alarming even one puffin or razorbill. Not until dusk, when the seabirds subsided, would he attempt the steep climb to the headland.

Abbie seemed more aware of Joellen's resentment than her father was. It was almost as if he refused to admit that things might not work out. So when Joellen told him that she wanted to take her things onto the island and spend the night there, he seemed genuinely surprised, taken aback. Abbie spoke up for her. It was just the kind of adventure she would have wanted when she was a kid.

They were eating an early supper to make up for no lunch and to give them as much time as they needed ashore after sundown. Dad was preoccupied, anxious to begin his egg and puffin count. Not that he could tell much this evening. It would take a few days to check every burrow and banded puffin. These were the ones that had been brought here as hatchlings five years ago.

They had been hand-reared until they were ready to flutter down to the water and swim out to sea. If the project worked, this would be the first year that survivors would return to breed. Dad had set up puffin decoys to lure them and mirrors to hold their attention.

Two years ago Joellen had been out here with her parents, watching some of the native puffins strut in front of the first experimental mirrors. With those amazingly colorful parrot beaks and eye markings that gave them such an air of surprise, they had looked like cartoon penguins in formal dress as they bowed to their reflections. It had been hard for Joellen and Mom and Dad to smother laughter.

"You'll keep clear of the mirrors?" Dad reminded Joellen.

"Of course." Wasn't he even slightly concerned about her being alone up there?

"Take a snack with you," Abbie suggested, "in case you get hungry or thirsty."

"All I need is my notebook and pencil," Joellen retorted. "And a flashlight." She knew she'd regret turning down Abbie's suggestion.

No more dumb moves, she told herself, as she reached into the forward cabin for her sleeping bag and and down vest. When no one was looking, she would grab some cookies and an orange or whatever she could stuff into her knapsack.

Landing was always tricky at Fowlers Island. Even when the wind was down, there was a sea swell to contend with. Dad rowed strongly toward the slipway, which still had a cable that could be winched to the top of the cliff. With the boat bobbing and slapping the water, he attached his loaded seabag to the cable hook. Then he shoved the dinghy aft. Joellen grabbed the foot of the ladder that was bolted to the rock face.

"Abbie first," he directed.

Joellen climbed after her. She knew the routine here. Dad would secure the oars and then haul the empty dinghy right out of the water behind him. It was the only way to keep it from slamming into the rock. She kept on climbing until the iron ladder curved up over the edge of the cliff. Abbie extended a hand, which Joellen ignored. She knew how to roll free of the ladder and onto the cliff edge, rolling once more to make room for Dad behind her.

He went straight to the cable and winched the heavy seabag up to the top.

"Neat!" Abbie exclaimed.

Dad grinned. "You should've seen it when the Coast Guard manned the lighthouse. They'd come out for you in one of their boats and then wait for the right wave to lift it onto the rails. Then the guy on top would haul up the boat with its passengers." He dragged the bag across the thick turf and opened it. "Nothing high tech about that operation, but it worked."

"Did having the Coast Guard so close to the nesting site drive the puffins off?"

Dad shook his head. "By the time the Coast Guard moved in, the damage was already done. Puffins were an easy catch. They were wiped out by egg and bird hunters in the last two centuries."

"I don't get it," Abbie said. "Why didn't the puffins come back when the hunting stopped?"

"It's the old safety-in-numbers problem. When only a few nesting pairs remain, there's no security. And now the great black-backed gulls have taken the place of humans as the most efficient predators. Also, there's the sheep. They do a lot of damage to the fragile turf here where the puffins burrow."

By now they had reached the first mirror. Dad motioned to Abbie and Joellen to stand back while he examined the surrounding turf. "See?" he said on a rising note of irritation as he kicked aside a pile of sheep droppings. "We need a fence across the island to keep the sheep away from here."

"Can that be done?" asked Abbie.

Dad shook his head again. "And what really bugs me," he said, "is that the blackberries and alders grow so thick across the spine of the island that you have to bushwhack your way if you want to get across. Only the sheep manage to come and go. They tunnel through all that undergrowth. There's nothing to hold them back. We didn't have enough funding to pay the guy that grazes these islands to take his sheep off for a few years—at least until the puffin population is reestablished."

Dad was still describing the problem and complaining when Joellen took her sleeping bag and other gear up toward the lighthouse. She found a spot free of anything that was likely to smell bad and spread out her things. Dad's voice faded and then emerged again, coming now from farther along the cliff edge. He sounded calmer, and there was an ebb and flow to his speech, with pauses as Abbie responded on an eager but soothing note.

Joellen opened her notebook and peered at yesterday's writing. Although Mom had given her the notebook so that she could keep a journal in it, Joellen had found herself beginning a story instead, a real story taking place in olden times, of all things.

She had no idea why or how she had come up with a background calling for old-fashioned clothes and boats and tools and stuff. It just seemed right somehow. At least it proved that she was writing about someone entirely made up, even if the person was a girl about her age. Joellen figured that as she wrote, she would eventually discover who the girl was and what would become of her.

"Josie! Josie?" Dad sounded anxious. He must have been calling for a while.

"What?" she called back through the dusk. "Don't call me Josie."

"I didn't know where you were," he said, his voice coming closer.

"Here," she said, flashing her light his way. "Right here."

She could tell that he had stopped. "You sure you don't want to sleep aboard?"

"Sure," she told him. "See you in the morning," she added, wondering who would have the stronger pull on him at dawn, Abbie or the puffins.

When she could hear him no longer, she bent over her notebook and wrote: "She would never see her mother again." She erased "mother" and wrote "father" in its place. "The sea would be his grave, cold and indifferent." She stared at this last word with surprise and pleasure. She didn't think she had ever used it before. Maybe she had never even heard it spoken. It had just come to her the way events might unfold if she gave the "she" of the story breathing room to grow into someone with a name and features that so far remained blank.

All at once Joellen knew that in her story a boat had

foundered and broken up. In the olden days there were lots of shipwrecks. Nowadays everyone had all kinds of aids to navigation. But back before loran and radar, before engines and automated light signals, ships would lose their direction and run onto ledges. Even within sight of land, but with no way to reach it. How had one girl made landfall when everyone else had perished? Well, maybe someone had managed to save her and then drowned while returning to the shipwreck to rescue someone else.

Think of the girl, shivering and exhausted, watching the tide rising up over the ledges and still rising, until the sea took each and every one of the remaining survivors.

"No," Joellen murmured, starting to erase what she had written. Not that it was wrong. It was just that she had gotten ahead of her story. Now, as the first scene came clear, she saw that she had to begin anew. "No. Noo," she moaned as she rubbed until the paper began to tear.

And from somewhere in the woods an owl called, "Oo-ooo."

5

Chris couldn't help thinking that if he turned back now, it would be a kind of defeat. Besides, making his way to the lighthouse was a statement about where he stood, which was now, in the present.

Grandad held on to the past. The tragic accident of Grandad's childhood that had robbed him of his mother and brother was still a part of his life. But for Chris it was only a sad story to which Grandad attached some evil significance. It was understandable. Two disasters affecting the same family and occurring on or near one island could lead to weird conclusions.

All the same, real dangers lurked here, too. Chris had been taught to respect the natural hazards of sea cliffs and steep tides, especially under a darkening sky. The light faded so slowly at this season that you could lose track of time. Still, when the moon rose, it would be nearly full. The sea would reflect and magnify it.

Chris knew that his parents would have told him to stick to an inland path. Last time he had followed the shoreline all the way around the island, neither Mom nor Dad had known exactly where he was until he had shown up at the cellar hole. It was one of those rare times before Sue got married when the whole family was together for a long weekend. Mom, who usually worked Saturdays in the gift shop, had taken off because she liked to make a point about Fowlers' being just like any other island, except that it had a lighthouse on it. She used to worry when Chris was little and spent so much time out on Spars Island with Grandad during the summer months when she was needed in the shop almost every day. Dad figured Chris would eventually figure things out for himself. Just because he liked to listen to Grandad spin his yarns about the old-timers who fished and quarried around these islands didn't mean he'd swallow all the garbage about curses and jinxes.

Chris paused to watch the water far below slosh into a rocky crevice. He guessed that the tide had turned. He had about three hours to return this way before the sea covered these boulders.

He kept on until the way became so steep that he had to use his hands to keep from sliding. Enough of that, he thought. It never was fun landing in the drink. Not that he couldn't grab some rockweed and haul himself out again. But getting wet tonight would be downright miserable.

For a while he kept to the sheep path that wound along the edge of the cliff. He was so intent on watching where he put his feet that he didn't even notice that he had reached Dread Mans Cove until he heard the sea pounding in and then sucking back with that rustling sound that Grandad used to call the rattle of bones. Only those were stones the water rolled, not bones. The noise was usually loudest on a rising tide because the water lifted the stones from beneath while the receding waves tumbled them seaward.

Chris stopped to look down. Night was closing the space between the facing headlands. Somehow the gathering dark only deepened the drop. A solitary gull banked downward and landed on a ledge below. All Chris could see of it was a white smudge on black rock, but he could hear an outcry, shrill and brief. Probably the gull had invaded some other gull's space. He tried not to think about the times he had witnessed one gull grabbing another's chick. Brutal birds, especially the blackbacks. Cannibals. He didn't think he could ever stomach eating gulls' eggs. He would stick to the eggs of clean, fish-eating birds like puffins.

It was too late now to do any useful exploring. What did he hope to find anyway? So many people had scavenged here since the Coast Guard had given up its station on Fowlers that there couldn't be much left. Still, the search for anything that might be useful was likely to be his sole entertainment this week. Supper tonight, mussels and clams steamed in rockweed, had been filling but not too satisfying. Butter would have made a difference; potatoes would have helped. If he could find a can or, better still, a pot without holes, he would be able to cook up a chowder of sorts.

The sheep path turned away from the cove. Here the dense growth of young alders forced him to strike out on his own. That didn't worry him. Sooner or later he would pick up his path, or another one. Anyway, he knew where he was heading. Any moment now he would catch his first glimpse of the lighthouse.

Rethinking the timing, he quickened his pace. If worse came to worst, he could spend the night in the sheep pen cellar hole, although he would have to backtrack into the woods to get enough spruce branches to use as a cover.

25

On he went, brambles grabbing at his ankles until he kicked himself free. But here was the path again, and it was more open. He could feel the wind and hear the surf. And there was the lighthouse beam shining way out over the water and then vanishing.

All that he could see now was a faint glimmer on the black surface of the sea. In a few seconds the beam would return. But what had happened to the moon? It seemed to be swathed in rags, scraps of cloud shredding into mist. The air was different, too. He zipped up his jacket and dug his hands into his pockets.

There was no hurry now. He was definitely stuck on this end of the island tonight.

He was still some distance from the point when a tiny light flickered on, off, and then on again. He stopped in his tracks. The light, quite close to the ground, was unconnected to the lighthouse. He glanced skyward. Maybe this was a trick of the patchy moonlight reflected on a bit of glass. Chris imagined Grandad hanging back from that fitful light. It would be cool to come up with an obvious and provable source that would blow away the sinister notions grown men and women passed on from one generation to the next.

But when the wind carried an almost human sound his way, Chris was brought up short. The skin between his shoulder blades tightened as if hit by a sudden chill. He told himself he had to stop in order to hear without interference from his footsteps or his jacket brushing against the brittle stalks of last fall's goldenrod. He held his breath, waited, and then exhaled. He must have imagined that moan. It showed how ghostly stories could worm their way into your mind.

Striding on into the wind, he thought he heard the sound again, muted like an echo. He couldn't be sure.

6

At first light of day the birds seemed to wake all at once in a burst of clamorous cries. Enough to raise the dead, thought Joellen. Where had she heard that phrase? What had put it into her head?

Rolling onto her back, she watched the dark and light shapes of gulls in flight. Then she sat up, the sleeping bag still drawn tight. She would have to get closer to the cliff edge for a glimpse of her father's boat on its mooring. But she could see beyond that to the bare dome of Parsons Sham, where terns darted and swooped and fought off hungry gulls.

She knew that one of the reasons Dad objected to the sheep here was that they disturbed birds like guillemots and terns that laid their eggs in the open. When terns used to nest on Fowlers's headland, they harried the gulls that preyed on exposed eggs and chicks. But now the fierce little terns raised their chicks on Parsons Sham, and that left the puffins and razorbills at the mercy of the gulls.

A couple of years ago she had taken off after a great blackback that snatched up a baby gull. Screaming and yelling, she had flung her boot at it, but the black-backed gull had simply lifted into the air with the chick dangling and still flailing a scrawny wing. Even Mom couldn't bear to watch the gulls whacking and mangling chicks they consumed. But she understood why Dad never intervened. At least she said she did. It was only through observing behaviors that the impact of population surges on more fragile species could be monitored.

Monitoring meant keeping a low profile while watching the killing. What kind of a person could do that? A person who worked with a kind of concentration that sealed out everything else. Yet Dad could also be so different. How many times had he reached into a burrow to extract a nestling bird, always careful, gentle. He had taught Joellen how to cup a downy chick in her hands without injuring or even frightening it. The baby puffins they had imported from Newfoundland to bring new life to the dying colony here on Fowlers Island had to be fed and, finally, banded before they fledged and went to sea.

Dad and Mom and their small team of workers had restored old burrows and dug new ones and then raised the orphan chicks through every kind of weather. In between there had been visits to Parsons Sham to count terns and black guillemots and tiny storm petrels, some even nesting on the lonely Sham Rock, which reared up to the east like a lonely sentinel, belled to warn off ships approaching in the fog.

Fog. The wind had changed overnight. Joellen could feel

the moisture carried on southeasterly air flows. She was glad she had her down vest.

By the time she was up and had her sleeping bag rolled, she was wearing everything she had off the boat, including her foul-weather jacket. She made her way to the edge of the cliff above the mooring. Usually Dad would be out by now, but the hatch covers were still pulled shut. She thought about shouting down to him. She would have to get his attention before he came ashore to be sure he brought along her extra sweater. And did she need to remind him not to forget her breakfast? It wasn't like him to stay aboard after daylight. If Abbie could make him forget what he was here for, she might also make him forget that his daughter was practically stranded on this island.

Instead of calling down to the silent boat, she pulled her notebook and pencil out from her knapsack and drew up her knees. She began to write: "The girl did not yet know that she had been abandoned." Joellen frowned. She wasn't exactly sure whether the girl would have seen the others drown and the boat go under. Maybe she had simply woken up on a deserted shore. "She believed that it was only a matter of time until the boat hove in sight. Then she would hear voices and the snapping of sails let loose and the rattle of fittings as the sails dropped to the deck. Soon now someone would remember her and come with . . ." Joellen faltered. If her story took place in the days of sail, what kind of food would someone bring to the girl left stranded on the island? Sea biscuits, she decided, racking her brains; fish chowder.

All at once she recalled one time when *Dovekie*, waiting out a storm, had been tied up alongside a trawler. The fishermen had invited Mom and Dad and Joellen aboard for a breakfast of fresh herring rolled in oatmeal and fried in butter. Mom and Dad had contributed good bread from home.

Joellen could almost smell that breakfast now and feel the heat from the stove and hear the stories told back and forth across the crowded table where they all sat snug and safe from the howling wind and lashing rain. Afterward Mom had offered to make the fishermen chowder for their dinner. They had contributed halibut and cod. Mom had cooked on their stove, because it was bigger, but she had brought over other things for making the huge pot of soup that was like the ocean in its variety, but with plenty of onions and carrots and potatoes to go with the fish.

Joellen resumed writing. She described the food the girl might expect to be brought. And what would she be wearing? What kind of protection would she have against the weather? Joellen wished she knew more about old-fashioned clothes. "She huddled under her shawl," wrote Joellen, "but it was hard to move about on the dangerous bird cliffs with her long skirt catching in tufts of grass and her shawl slipping whenever she had to use her hands to break free of brambles."

There weren't any brambles right here, but who knew what it was like years ago? Anyway, there were plenty of brambles inland among the black alders.

Just to try it out, Joellen shed her foul-weather jacket and down vest. She slid her arms out of her sleeves to give her sweatshirt a sort of shawl effect. She kept the hood open on her head. It certainly wasn't very good protection. Someone left like this could die from hypothermia. Almost everyone in olden times must have frozen to death. It was amazing that anyone survived.

She glanced down at the boat again and realized that

within the last few minutes the fog had moved closer. It was creepy how fast it could cut you off. Any kid would feel abandoned if she woke up to find herself all alone in a place like this. But imagine having to deal with fog before radio direction finders and radar and depth-sounding devices. Imagine if no one knew she was here. Or even alive.

The fog signal had begun its mournful, rhythmic warning.

Crawling and climbing, she hauled herself up onto more level ground and nearly struck one of the mirrors Dad had told her to stay away from. Up here the moist breeze quickly chilled her. She wrapped the sweatshirt arms around her neck and then realized to her dismay that she had left her foul-weather jacket somewhere below on one of the shelves of the cliff. Not far, of course. She had pretty much hugged the upper area. Still, the fog now covered the entire headland. Maybe if she stretched out on her stomach and leaned way over and fished around, she could reach her things from here.

She wasn't alarmed. Even though she couldn't see the boat anymore, she knew that she would hear Dad and Abbie speak when they came out of the cabin. Joellen still had plenty of time to get herself sensibly dressed before Dad saw her. She needed to give every appearance of being responsible if he was going to let her stay out here another night, especially in the fog.

So she played it safe, keeping her body firmly grounded as she groped as far as she could reach along the next level down. Pebbles and bits of shell scattered. It occurred to her that she must have been fairly close to the mirror when she had taken off her jacket and vest. Dragging one hand, she slithered forward until the mirror presented itself, unseen, as a smooth, hard barrier. Good. Now all she had to do was dangle headfirst and she would probably be able to see her things.

As she inched forward, leaning down, both arms free, the hood dropped over her head. She shrugged it back. But now her hair was a tangled screen in front of her eyes, some strands, beaded with droplets of fog, plastered to her face. She had to rely on her touch, not sight. And there they were, her jacket and vest. Clutching them in one hand, she pushed herself up and back until she could roll away from the cliff edge and be sure of solid ground.

She had forgotten how spongy the soil could be up here where it was undermined by burrows. Mindful now that the entire cliff edge was riddled with them, she scrambled farther back before stopping to put her sweatshirt on properly and to pull on her outerwear. Already the down vest felt damp and cold.

7

Chris decided to lie low and see which burrows, if any, were visited by puffins or razorbills. There wasn't much activity yet. If he could feel the fog drifting in from the sea before it actually arrived, probably the birds did, too. Maybe they were waiting for it to give them some protection against the gulls.

He hadn't bargained on fog. He hoped it didn't last long. In July and August it could hang around for a week or two at a time.

Figuring that he could conceal himself if he kept low, he made his way to the westernmost extent of the bird headland, where the shelving cliff provided a natural stairway down. It wasn't far from the iron ladder and boat slipway.

Scanning the area, he caught his breath at the sight of a

yacht made fast to the mooring left by the Coast Guard. No sign of life, though. Probably the people had every kind of navigational aid inside their cabin and had known of the incoming fog. Nothing to do but sleep in on a morning like this.

He descended at an angle until he could settle more or less comfortably beside a protruding boulder. If anyone came out of the boat into the cockpit, Chris would see the person long before the person would discover him. All he would have to do was shrink against the stone. Anyway, the fog was getting closer. The horn already announced its coming in deep, muffled notes. Pretty soon nothing would be visible unless it was as close as the puffin that whirred overhead, its stubby wings beating like a bumblebee's. It came to rest somewhere higher up on the cliff face. By the time Chris stood tall to see, the puffin had disappeared into a burrow.

He waited awhile longer. No other puffin flew into view. Then, just as he was about to move to a better vantage point, one emerged beyond the boulder. That was lucky. He might be able to explore the hole without being attacked. He had heard that those brilliantly colored puffin bills could deliver a mean bite.

He edged closer to the boulder. Startled, the puffin raised its wings. But it didn't take to the air. He froze. The puffin cocked its head, eyeing him. It looked more like a kid's toy than a living creature that flew thousands of miles over open water to hatch and rear its young on this smelly bit of turf and rock.

It struck him that he might actually be able to catch this one. But the thought of killing and eating it turned his stomach. He wasn't even sure he wanted an egg that would probably taste fishy. Still, if he marked any eggs he found today and then changed his mind tomorrow or the next day, he would have that option.

Slowly he moved toward the hole until the boulder forced him outward. He couldn't help dislodging loose, pebbly soil. The puffin ducked its head a few times and took a few penguinlike steps away from him. This wasn't bad. If he could block the puffin's return, he would have a chance to reach into its burrow.

While the puffin teetered on the edge of the cliff, he thrust in his arm. It wasn't long enough to get to the nest. He would have to widen the opening so that he could get his whole shoulder inside or try another burrow. But there might not even be an egg there. All that work for nothing?

He decided to move on while he could still see where he was going. The fog had all but obliterated the boat. He could wander the cliff face unseen by any of the people on the yacht. But not by the puffin. The moment he straightened, it took off. A rising clamor of gulls made note of its flight or maybe of a mate returning with fish. The little bird had vanished.

He had to feel his way along the turf shelf, gradually climbing upward as he faced east, the fog like fine rain against his face.

Telling himself that he could come back later armed with a stick for digging, he gave up the egg hunt. Right now he would settle for a fire and leftover mussels. It would take him a good fifteen minutes, maybe as much as a half hour, to get back to his campsite and his stack of wood. At this rate it was going to be a long, long week.

If the fog didn't lift, he might even be tempted to quit when Andy and Eric showed up midweek. But if the fog didn't lift, would they they take that crummy boat out here to Fowlers Island with its ledges and treacherous currents? He had promised Grandad that someone would check up on him and report back. If no word came, he wouldn't put it past Grandad to conclude that Chris had been swallowed whole by the island ghost girl.

Probably something real was behind all that curse stuff. Even Dad admitted that when he was growing up on Spars Island, all the old-timers claimed that ever since Keeper Fossett had deserted the lighthouse, something that happened so long ago it was just a blurred memory, anyone with a drop of Fossett blood in his veins had better steer clear of Fowlers.

No one seemed to know where the ghost idea came from. But Grandad said that when he was growing up, his grandmother sometimes spoke of a girl who walked the shoreline of Fowlers and looked out over the dangerous waters surrounding the island. Grandad wasn't clear about why the girl was there. Maybe his grandmother never told him, or maybe he had just forgotten. By the time he passed this island lore on to his son and grandson, the girl had long since become a ghost in the minds of Grandad's cronies.

Chris's dad had been able to blow off all that superstition by simply leaving it behind with Grandad on Spars. And after years of managing sheep on islands hereabouts without any serious mishaps, Dad had proved that Fowlers was no different from any other island.

Once when Grandad was running off at the mouth about the Fowlers Island curse, Chris had remarked that it was too bad they couldn't wake the dead for an hour or so to clear up some of their family history. Grandad had just about hit the ceiling. "Don't ever say that again," he had railed at Chris. "Don't even think it."

It was the first time Chris had understood how deeply the past haunted Grandad. And not so much the known past as the past that had come down to him through stories and notions his grandmother had raised him on.

Chris paused to listen for signs of life aboard the yacht. Was it possible that the yacht crew had already rowed ashore? With all the bird clamor around the headland and the fog signal going, he wasn't likely to hear subdued voices unless they were directly upwind. The last thing he wanted was to bump into someone who might ask a lot of questions. He didn't want to have to explain himself.

He picked his way, seeking handholds where the turf felt firm. When he reached the top of the cliff, he would be completely exposed, at least so far as anyone could be seen through this pea soup.

So why did he have a feeling that he was being watched? He couldn't shake off the sense of another presence. It made his heart pound and his breath come short.

He stopped for a moment. As he reached up with his left hand, his knuckles struck something smooth and upright. He recoiled. Then he realized it must be one of those fool mirrors that he'd heard about. Some scientist from away had put them up, along with decoys, to lure puffins that had been artificially reared and fledged from here. The mirrors and decoys were supposed to keep the puffins around long enough for others to come, breed, and make more puffins. All of Ledgeport knew about this project. It prompted a whole slew of jokes about getting into trouble with mirrors.

Coming up against the obvious put things back in perspective. Chris raised himself on his elbows and turned, so that he could peer directly at the mirror. There was its surface, blurred by fog. Resting on his right elbow, he made one swipe with his left hand. It cleared a swath through the moisture, which instantly started to fog up again.

He was still too low to see himself reflected, but something else seemed to be there. He strained to raise himself a bit higher. He could only support himself this way for a heartbeat. Was the mirror showing a tangle of black hair tumbling out from under some kind of cloak or shawl? He couldn't hold his position long enough to be sure. But he would have sworn that was what he had glimpsed.

Sliding back from the ledge, he drew up his knees, which felt bruised from carrying his weight on the stones and shells that lined the cliff shelf. He swiveled so that he could look up to his right. That was where the person must be whose reflection showed in the fogging mirror. He couldn't make out anything, anyone. He stared and stared. Forgetting to be cautious, he shifted backward to position himself more directly beneath the person. Then he raised himself again. No one.

Baffled, he waited a moment. What did he expect to find? Certainly not a girl in an old-fashioned shawl. He shut his eyes against the gray, wet world. What exactly had he seen? A person or a picture of a person?

He shivered. Time enough to consider all this once he was back across the island warming himself at a fire. Backing away, he groped for a fresh firm grip on the turf. He didn't feel like hauling himself anywhere near that mirror again.

8

"Josie! Josie!" The voice calling barely penetrated the baffle of fog and the gulls screeching and wailing overhead.

Joellen turned, suddenly bewildered. It was something like those birthday party games from when she was little, pin the tail on the donkey or blindman's bluff, where you couldn't see and were made to feel confused and everyone teased you.

"Don't call me Josie!" she shouted.

"Well, where are you?" Dad's voice sounded clearer now, calmer.

"Here," she answered. "I'm not sure." She had thought she was heading for the lighthouse. But when she stopped to put on her vest and foul-weather jacket, she sort of lost her bearings. She took a few experimental steps until she could feel solid rock underfoot. She was pretty sure of her location now. "On the lookout place," she called to her father, using the name they had given the outcrop in the days when her parents had established safety boundaries for her while they fed the transplanted puffin chicks.

"Stay there," he ordered. "Wait."

Then he and Abbie loomed through the fog, indistinct and somehow gigantic until they stood before her.

"It's a lot thicker than I expected," Dad said. "I was afraid you might be on the cliff."

"If I had been," Joellen retorted, "all that yelling could've blown me off. I can't imagine what it did to the puffins."

"What's eating you?" he demanded. "It was your idea to stay here overnight, not mine."

"And I loved it," she retorted. "I was fine. It was peaceful," she added, not finishing the thought: until you came.

"We brought breakfast," Abbie said. "You must be starving." She held out a thermos and an insulated bag.

Unwilling to admit that she was dying for something hot, Joellen thanked her. First she drank some cocoa. Then she gobbled an apple muffin.

"There's a container of oatmeal with maple syrup," Abbie told her. "And I brought your heavy sweater, just in case. It's in John's pack."

Joellen nodded. She wished Abbie wouldn't try so hard with her, but she had to admit that Dad probably wouldn't have supplied her this well. She squatted down to examine the contents of his pack, which included candy bars, cans of juice, sandwich stuff, toilet paper, and all his materials for recording observations and keeping his census. She did not remark on the futility of high-powered binoculars and telephoto lenses in fog as dense as this.

Dad and Abbie took some things from the pack and made off for the cliff. "Where will you be?" he thought to call back to Joellen.

"I don't know. Around. Why?"

"Well," he responded lamely, "it's lousy visibility."

"No kidding."

"Jos—Joellen! I'm serious. I don't want you anywhere dangerous alone."

She nodded.

"Did you hear me?"

"Yes."

"Why don't we agree to meet here at noon?" Abbie suggested.

Joellen glowered into the fog. Why couldn't Dad see through Abbie's angel routine?

"Okay?" Dad asked.

"Sure. Fine," Joellen said to him.

She had no plan. She had nowhere to go. And they would be stuck here until the fog lifted, the three of them. Some vacation!

At least she had shown that she was perfectly capable of taking care of herself without being cooped up with them in *Dovekie*. Maybe she could clean out a space in the lighthouse for tonight. Would Dad let her? The main entrance was boarded up because the lighthouse was supposed to be off-limits, but Dad's team had used it for shelter more than once. There was a way into the lighthouse around to the side where slanting doors could be pulled up from the ground. First you had to go down and cross the dark cellar to stairs that led to the main room.

She picked her way with care. Even trying to avoid nests, she nearly trod on a speckled chick huddled in a chink in the ledge. The baby gull blended right in with spattered rock. Joellen scootched down to gaze at it. She knew it wouldn't budge until its parent came to it with food. She looked skyward in case one was heading her way, but the fog blotted out the winged forms. There was just the continuous clamor overhead. Anyway, there was no way of telling what kind of errand a gull was on when it did swoop down. It could as easily kill the chick as feed it.

Straightening, she moved on. First she had to get her flashlight out of her pack. Then she headed for the slanting doors. Thank goodness they weren't padlocked. But it took all her strength to pull up one side. It was always a bit creepy descending the stone steps. The air was stale as well as cold, what she imagined a tomb would feel like.

She hurried to the inside stairs, lighting her way into the round room she was familiar with from earlier years. Dad had stored some equipment here. "PUFFIN PROJECT" was printed in heavy marker across the top of two cartons. The marks on the floor showed where the backup generator used to be kept. There really wasn't much to look at here, especially now that someone had wiped off most of the graffiti.

A few years ago the circular wall had been covered with messages, most of them dirty, with one or two good rhymes that you weren't allowed to repeat. Dad said the writing had to be recent, since the Coast Guard shut down, except for the carved face with the words *Kilroy Was Here* gouged in the first riser of the stairs that led to the tower. That one might date all the way back to World War II. Dad said you couldn't blame guys on duty for going stir-crazy and needing something to do besides playing cards. But Mom had replied that nothing could excuse the sexist scrawlings.

Imagine living here for years and years. Of course in olden times there was a house and barn with chickens and a cow and sheep. Joellen sank to the floor beside her pack and pulled out her pad and pencil. She stared at the story she had started. So far nothing had happened in it. Except the shipwreck. Probably nothing much did ever happen here long ago, only a boring routine for the lightkeeper and his family. No television or radio. Did they have books?

Joellen wished the old house still existed. It would be something to explore. Dad said it had been torn down when the Coast Guard took over and built living quarters for the men on duty here. Even that building was gone now, except for the ruins of two foundation walls. Nothing whole remained but this stone lighthouse. If anything had lasted from when a single family farmed while keeping the light here, someone would have taken it by now. It would probably be worth a lot as an antique.

Joellen reread her nonstory. If a girl were abandoned here, then it had to be in a time when there was no lighthouse or farm, or else she wouldn't be alone. Of course it didn't have to be this exact same island unless something had happened to the lightkeeper and his family. What if some disaster had wiped them out? Now this had possibilities.

The girl would find an empty house. Maybe there would be food left, too. No one would know she was there, the sole survivor of a shipwreck. What if the lightkeeper had gone to his death trying to rescue the other passengers? Maybe his last words were instructions for keeping the light, and the girl was the only person who could carry on. Which of course she would do because she owed her life to him.

Anyway, the girl wouldn't want another boat to stray onto these treacherous rocks. Even if she didn't have a clue to what had become of the other passengers in her boat, she would have a clear memory of how it had tilted helplessly on its vicious granite bed while the wild, angry sea pounded it to bits.

Bending over the pad, Joellen wrote and wrote. Here was drama at last.

9

Chris waited for the fire to die down before going to look for the bawling sheep. He tried to tell himself that it was just a fluke that he was here and heard her. Most island sheep in trouble either got themselves out of it or died.

Dad always said that was the trade-off for island sheep. A ewe that had made it through a hard winter, especially if she dropped a live lamb or two come spring and then had to nurse them, might not be strong enough to fight her way out of trouble.

This would be the first year Chris could remember not going out to the islands with Dad. He would have to handle the shearing and vaccinating on his own, unless Mom could get some more time away from the shop to help him.

Chris didn't mind the sheep work as long as Dad was

around to make the decisions and deal with the bad situations. If this ewe he'd heard hollering as he came across the island had a lambing problem, he wasn't sure he would be able to handle it. Funny thing was that he hadn't always minded that sort of mess. When he was little, it had never bothered him the way it did now.

He kicked the end of a log that had only burned in the middle. One end flared up. He knew he was just putting off going to see what was wrong with the ewe. But she was quiet for the moment. Maybe if he waited awhile longer, she would stop for good. It would probably mean she had been calling a lamb and had just found it, something as simple as that.

He dug through the cooling rockweed that he had steamed the mussels in and found one last morsel to eat. He wasn't really hungry anymore, but he wasn't satisfied either. He wondered what the people on the yacht had had for breakfast.

High above the beach an osprey whistled its plaintive call. It sounded like a person crying, "Save me," even though it was probably just going fishing. "Bring me a nice mackerel," Chris said, wondering whether ospreys ever did lose their prey and what the chances would be that this hawk would drop its catch right on his rockweed fry pan. From somewhere inland another osprey answered the first. And then, as if reminded of her plight, the ewe took to bawling again.

Groaning, Chris rose and headed for the woods. Anyway, he told himself, it was real; it was something he knew about, not an imaginary presence he couldn't see.

It took longer than he expected. The fog was thinner in the woods, but he had to fight the tangled undergrowth every step of the way. Each time he thought he was approaching a clearing, he would find a huge tree trunk blocking him. He had never seen so many fresh blowdowns.

"All right," he shouted at the sheep somewhere ahead of him. Then he walked into an impenetrable wall of branches. Not spruce. He had to back up and look for a way around. This was one mighty big oak, and from the look of it, it hadn't been down all that long.

The sheep was so close he could smell her. But the tree wouldn't let him near. In the end he had to skirt the entire area and come around from the opposite direction. He was sliding down toward the immense root system when he saw the sheep in the cavity left by the oak. She had probably led her lamb into it for shelter and then become trapped. The uprooted tree had ripped apart the subsoil and left it crumbly. She couldn't climb out.

His first thought was to go back for the rope. Then he took a closer look at the lamb, which stood humpbacked, a sign of being chilled or hungry. How long had they been down there? How long had the ewe gone without food?

He looked around for something to offer her. Moss was the only thing at hand, so he grabbed fistfuls and dropped some down to her. She gobbled it right up. Okay. So she was hungry. The rope would have to wait while he fed her. And what about water? Rockweed would help. He could bring some back from the shore. But she needed food right away, so he ripped off spruce branches and threw them down for the ravenous ewe. She cleaned off all the green needles and even some twigs.

No need for panic, he realized. She could be kept alive for quite a while this way. When he went to get rockweed, he could look for some drift he might use to free her and her lamb. He had already set aside a pallet that had washed ashore and the top of a lobster crate. Could he construct a sort of platform or ramp for her?

Now that he had a project, he felt a whole lot better about this stupid fix he was in. All at once he was full of energy and purpose. He could practically feel the fog clear out of his thoughts, too.

10

By midday Dad and Abbie had had enough of the fog and were glad for a break. Drenched and cold, they considered returning to the boat to warm up, then settled for lunch in the lighthouse. If the fog didn't lift, they would knock off work well before dark.

"Not that you can call what we're trying to see through light," Abbie remarked. "It's so gray that I keep thinking my glasses are dirty." She shrugged off her jacket and folded it carefully so that its wet outside didn't touch the inside.

Dad kept his on. When he rummaged for the bread and cheese, his sleeves dripped inside the bag.

Joellen noticed that Abbie noticed this. Mom would have said something about Dad's getting everything wet, but Abbie refrained from comment. Love, thought Joellen, amused and annoyed all at the same time. Love or insecurity. She wished the two of them had gone back to the boat.

"It does slow us down," Dad said. He was still talking about the fog. "But it's always so much more bearable when we know it's going to lift."

"Is it?" asked Joellen, spreading peanut butter on her bread.

Dad nodded. "Of course they were wrong about it in the first place. They didn't predict that it would come down this far. Still, the wind will be shifting sometime tomorrow. Being able to see will certainly speed up the census."

He and Abbie began to compare notes on their morning count. This was too familiar to Joellen. Until this year it had always been her mother's head bent over records next to Dad's. Joellen cut a chunk of cheese, stuffed some raisins into her pocket, and strode to the stairs.

But she didn't really want to go outside. She just wanted to get away from the sight of them together.

After returning for her flashlight, she went down to the cellar to poke around. First she played the light across the ceiling. There were still two filthy bulbs in sockets connected by a cable that cut across the space. Someone had used the cable for a clothesline. There was actually a sock hanging over it and other stuff, wire and rubber and old potwarp, rope that was used to connect lobster traps to buoys. She ducked lower than she needed to make sure she didn't touch that gross sock. Farther back she came to something that had once been white but was encrusted and stained. It might have been the tub part of an old-fashioned washing machine, except that it was too thick. She tried to shove it aside but couldn't budge it.

Footsteps on the stairs brought her up short. Maybe they

were going back to work and she would be left in peace with the food bag.

But it was just Abbie, toilet paper in hand, going out for obvious reasons. Joellen squeezed between the white thing and a metal frame and continued to explore. Her flashlight kept flickering. She would have to remember to put in fresh batteries.

"What are you looking for?" Abbie was back. Standing inside the bulkhead, she blocked the dim light that came from outdoors.

"Just looking," Joellen answered.

Abbie came toward her. "How did you get past—oh, I see." Without benefit of Joellen's flashlight, she managed to raise herself from the upper bar of the frame and vault over the white tub. "What's back here? I had no idea it went somewhere."

"It used to be a passage to the house. For bad weather. Dad said the other end collapsed a long time ago, so don't try going in."

"It can't hurt to go as far as it's open," Abbie said.

Right, thought Joellen, and when you get stuck in there and the roof caves in, I'll be a murder suspect. She directed the fading flashlight along the rough stonework that formed the foundation and the cellar wall. There were those stinky barrels, two of them propped side by side.

"Those look really old," Abbie said, turning back from the passage.

Joellen nodded. "They kept whale oil in them for the lighthouse."

"Really?" said Abbie. "Can you turn the flashlight this way? There's something painted on this end of the barrel."

Joellen obliged, although it didn't help much.

"One's an *S* and one's a *W*," Abbie said. "Hey, I think I know what they stand for: summer and winter. John," she called up to Joellen's dad, "guess what?"

With the flashlight practically useless, Joellen had no choice but to follow Abbie back upstairs. Dad had packed up the lunch things and was ready to go out to work. Fishing around for a package of cookies, Abbie jabbered on about early lighthouses, which used different weights of oil for warm or cold weather. She had been cruising on the Net to see what she could learn about this part of the coast and had stumbled on to an exhibition on Maine lighthouses. Even though she had moved on because she was really look-ing for natural history background, she had picked up some lighthouse information. "There's a big tank down there, too. It must have been for when they converted to kerosene. I'm surprised the wooden barrels were left."

Dad held out her jacket. "It would've been a big deal to move them," he said. "They're sort of built into the foundation now. Sometime or other it must've been rein-forced. The wall comes in around the far ends of the barrels. Should we leave the food in here out of the fog?"

"Yes," answered Joellen. "I might just have leftover stuff for supper."

"Oh, no," Dad told her. "You're coming back to the boat with us, at least for a hot meal. If you really want to spend another night up here, I'll row you to the ladder before dark."

Abbie didn't say anything. Probably she was relieved that she wouldn't have Joellen on the boat all night.

Joellen waited until they were gone before starting to write. Then she waited some more as she tried to coax a new idea to take shape in her head. The dangerous passage that led nowhere was distinctly ominous, especially if the house was still standing. It was the kind of place that made you think of some really horrible crime. What kind of murder might be committed in its dark recesses? Who would be the victim, who the murderer? And what would it have to do with a girl who was left alone to fend for herself? Would she even know where she was?

A nameless girl on a nameless island gave new meaning to being at sea.

11

Nothing worked. Nothing. When Chris tied one end of the rope to an arching oak root and took the other end down into the pit, the ewe went crazy. That was the problem with island sheep. They didn't trust you. Just being driven into a pen once or twice a year could send some of them into orbit. Even if he got her roped without strangling her or breaking her leg, she would keep on flailing until she had battered the lamb to death.

"Stupid," he muttered, looking down from the edge of the pit. Something that stupid deserved to die.

The ewe had backed her lamb against the opposite face of the pit. She was panting hard, a crazed gleam in her yellow eye.

"I fed you, didn't I? How come you can't tell that I'm trying to help you?"

The ewe turned her head, checked that the lamb was still back there, and stamped her forefoot at him.

"Great," he told her. "So be a stupid hero. Don't get yourself saved. Who cares?"

But he broke off some more spruce boughs to drop down to her before he left.

One thing about this failed rescue was that he didn't feel the need of a fire, not after tramping back and forth between the beach and the pit with armfuls of rockweed and kelp and some of the driftwood he'd collected. If anything, he was too hot.

The trouble was that he couldn't get the fool sheep out of his mind. No matter how he racked his brains, he couldn't think of a way to free her. What would Dad do? Well, not walk away from the situation. If he couldn't save a sheep, he would kill it rather than leave it to starve.

Chris tried to imagine hurling down a rock heavy enough to crack her skull. Yeah, right, he thought. Like she'd stand there for him, not moving. Well, he had a knife. So he could slide back in there, tackle her, and cut her throat. And that would leave just the lamb to deal with. Easy enough.

He was so disgusted he couldn't even think about picking mussels before high tide. How could he muster an appetite after inventing those grisly scenarios?

So he decided to go back to the lighthouse end of the island. Maybe the yacht was gone now and he could scrounge around for puffin eggs. Not that he was hungry. But it would take his mind off the stupid sheep.

He thought the fog had thinned some because there was so much more visibility in the woods and even down around Orcutt Cove. But as he headed east along the foreshore, the fog thickened.

As soon as he reached the open slope of Folly Point, he walked into what felt like a solid wall of moisture. He must have startled sheep grazing on the point, although he never saw them. Still, he could hear their hooves clatter on table rock as they bolted somewhere behind him, probably heading for cover in the woods.

Farther on, as he traversed the edge of Dread Mans Cove, he made himself glance down. When he couldn't see a thing, he hung an arm around a sapling so that he could lean over. It struck him as odd that this cliff overhung its lower ledges, while on the headland the bird cliffs, with their natural steps, were just the opposite. He supposed it had something to do with centuries of wave action. Where Dread Mans Cove faced due east, exposed to the open sea, the bird cliffs presented a shoulder to the sea and looked more to the north, where Parsons Sham and Sham Rock broke the full assault of northeast gales.

Chris continued on the narrow trail. He felt more in control now that he had figured out a kind of scientific explanation for the different formations of this island's cliffs. Grandad, who knew more about the coast and islands than almost anyone around, got himself all fouled up by mixing fact and fiction. When you listened to him, you could never be sure what was real and what was laid on for effect or because he actually believed those tall tales.

The path skirted a dip in the turf. Maybe melting snow had flowed down through here. Chris tested the break in the path and decided to step across it rather than detour. The ground beneath his foot gave way. Grabbing wildly for the first thing he could reach, he lurched back and sideways, until he found himself splayed out, hugging a moss-covered trunk. He could feel its rottenness and knew that any moment now it could fall apart. So he crawled over it and onto the hard surface of the sheep path.

He took a moment to catch his breath. He didn't have to look at where he had been. He understood that he had tried to put his weight on a spot where running water had undermined the fragile network of roots and thin soil that gave an illusion of solid turf. The sheep knew this. Maybe they had learned the hard way after one had broken through and fallen to the rocks below. Talk about stupid. They were some smarter than he was.

Taking to their path, his heart still racing, he tried to pace himself. For the first time since leaving the trapped ewe and lamb, he could almost imagine her panic. For a split second back there he had felt the abyss open beneath him. He would have clawed at a feather in the air to save himself.

It occurred to him that he had a perfectly good reason to ask for help. If the yacht was still there, he could hail it. All he needed was one other person, provided the guy had an ounce of good sense and a little muscle. Chris would explain that the sheep on this island belonged to his father, who was away for three weeks. Then he could hitch a ride to wherever the yacht was going because once he had revealed himself and asked for help, all bets were off.

Just knowing he had a way out gave him courage. He wasn't alone anymore, not really. He was pretty sure no yachtsman would be fool enough to take off from a safe mooring in this fog. Of course the boat would be there.

But the closer he came to the headland, the less certain he was that he wanted to give up so early in the game. After all, he hadn't even looked around the lighthouse for more stuff to help haul that ewe out. And now that he was walking over solid ground again, everything, except the air, seemed brighter. He stopped to pick up a stick with a knobby root at one end. It might help him scoop an egg from a burrow.

To test his own soundness, he sought out the mirror that had given him such a turn. He didn't have too tough a time finding it because it was placed on the first shelf down from the edge of the cliff. He picked his way with care, not for fear of falling but to keep from treading on baby gulls.

Occasionally he stopped to listen for signs of human life, but the only sounds that came to him were the cries of birds he still couldn't see. Suddenly his appetite was back. It had returned with a vengeance. When he came to the mirror, he knew before he looked that he would find no apparition in its reflection.

Sure enough, he stared at his own face. There was nothing beyond or behind it, no wild-haired creature in a cloak, no one to make his skin go icy cold and his breath catch in his throat. So much for the ghost girl, he thought. Now for tomorrow's breakfast.

12

Joellen's father waited until she was off the ladder. Of course he couldn't see her anymore. Probably he figured that as long as she didn't come tumbling down with a splash, she must have made it safely to the top.

She couldn't hear him shove off, but the first strokes of his oars came to her. Then he was out of earshot, and there were only the bird cries above and all around. Hoisting her knapsack, which was stuffed to near bursting, she ambled off in the direction of the bird cliff. She was in no hurry to settle down inside the lighthouse, and she wanted to check out the visibility.

Was the fog already lifting? It seemed that way until she glanced down. She couldn't see the water. She had the feeling that the drop from the headland was bottomless. It made her want to stick closer to solid ground.

Lowering her knapsack, she settled down beside a burrow and looked around. She could actually see a few yards to either side. Was that a decoy off to the right? No, it was a razorbill. It looked so much like a penguin that she kept on staring for a while. Probably she ought to jot down its location and the time. There were so few razorbills that Dad usually recorded every sighting.

She kept her eye on the bird as she extracted her notebook and pencil. Glancing at her watch, she then tried to estimate the distance from the mirror to this burrow and from here to the razorbill. She stood up to get a better perspective, and at the edge of her sight something below caught her attention. She strained to see more than that glimpse. Was it a rock that looked like someone crouching? Lots of rocks gave that impression, especially in the fog.

But how could there be a rock that size protruding from the cliff?

She turned, fumbling for her flashlight, and out of the corner of her eye saw the razorbill dart into a hole. Turning back, she gaped as the rock was transformed into a person. She craned forward. A person holding a white egg.

"What are you doing?" she snapped.

"Jeez!" He staggered, his arms flailing. When he regained his balance, he faced her. "Who the hell are you?" he demanded. It was hard to tell much about a short girl wearing oversize foul-weather gear, her dark hair pulled back under a head scarf.

"That's a puffin egg," she told him. "Put it back."

"I'm going to," he said. "I'm just marking it."

Marking it? Was he one of Dad's assistants who had just somehow materialized here? Was there another project going on that she didn't know about?

He said, "You should think twice before you startle people in a place like this."

"Well, you startled me, too. I'm here with my father. And his . . . assistant. Do you know him, John Roth?"

The guy shook his head. He didn't look old enough to be on any kind of project, except maybe as a subject for study. With shaggy brown hair stuck to his long face and scrawny neck, he made her think of some nestling just emerged from its egg.

"Do you know it's against the law to interfere with these birds?" she told him.

"What law?" he snapped. "Who says?"

"This island's posted," she retorted. She had just blurted that out about its being against the law. At least there was a sign warning mariners away from the bird cliffs. "No one's allowed here now," she added. "Put that egg back before it's too late."

He stooped down. She couldn't see exactly what he was up to until he wielded a stick. "Hey, don't do that," she ordered. "You'll hurt the parent or break the egg or something."

"I didn't hurt anything," he answered. "The parent isn't even in there. So back off."

"What's the mark for?" she asked him as he climbed up to her level.

"It's how you tell which egg's fresh," he said. "If there's an unmarked egg in there tomorrow, it'll be mine."

"Great!" she exclaimed. "You don't even know that puffins lay only one egg?"

"No way. What about these nests up here?" He pointed at two speckled eggs.

"They're herring gulls. Puffins are different. That egg

61

you marked is all that one puffin will lay this spring. My father's waited five years for it."

"How come five years?"

"Because that's how long it takes for puffins to start reproducing." She told him about the puffin chicks brought from Newfoundland and hand-raised so that they would fledge from here and maybe return in five years to breed and raise young.

"I know all that." He glanced around. "So where's your father?" he asked. "On that yacht?"

"Yes. He'll be back here tomorrow morning. Or I can call him over right now if you don't believe me."

"No, I believe you. I guess I do." He paused. "So did he leave you here to guard the puffins or what?"

"I just like staying here by myself," she declared pointedly. When he didn't respond to this, she went on. "Who're you here with? Where's your boat?"

"I'm alone, too. There's no boat."

"You mean you got dumped?" This possibility made him interesting. "On purpose?"

He nodded.

"So where's your gear?"

"The other side of the island. Orcutt Cove."

She felt like going inside now, but she wasn't sure she wanted him to know where she was spending the night.

"You know where that is?" he asked.

"Sort of," she replied. "I've never been all around this island. What are you here for?"

He wasn't sure what to admit. He could say he and his dad looked after sheep on five different islands, including this one, but then she might ask him why his dad wasn't here. "I'm just hanging out," he said finally, "doing this like

survival thing. You know, like living off the land and stuff."
If only he could think of the things Gary from away had
said about Brimstone Island.

Her eyes widened. "For how long?"

He shrugged. "Till they come back for me."

"They?"

"My friends."

"Friends dumped you and left you to fend for yourself.
Where are your parents?"

"What difference does it make? Is this against the law,
too?"

It was her turn to shrug. "It just seems weird, that's all."

"Like tricking puffins, making them think they belong
here, is normal?"

"Well, they do belong. They did. There were thousands
of puffins here once." Was it thousands or hundreds? "Then
people came and killed them and stole their eggs. Like you
were about to do."

"Bull!"

"It's true. Everyone knows it. You can read about how
the puffins were wiped out because they were so easy to
catch." She was racking her brains, trying to dredge up facts
she had heard so many times she had stopped paying attention to them. "And the great auk, which got extinct because
people kept on killing it and using it and not caring." When
was that? How long ago?

"Well, you puffin savers may be sorry," he retorted. "You
get too many of any of these birds and they kill the trees.
Crap all over them. You should see Hog Island over between
Coombes and Spars where my grandad lives. Shags and her-
ons and gulls crowded there, and now all the trees are poi-
soned."

"That won't happen with the puffins. They don't go near the woods, so they won't hurt the trees."

They glared at each other. All at once they had run out of steam. Chris was thinking that it was too dark now to get back across to Orcutt Cove. He'd just as soon spend the night in the lighthouse, only not if this girl was going to be there. And now it was too dark to look for firewood.

Joellen was thinking that he wasn't to be trusted around here. "Why don't you eat gulls' eggs?" she asked him. "There's no shortage of gulls."

"It's only—" He broke off. She thought he was going to steal one of her precious puffin eggs after all. "Tell you what," he said. "I'll promise to leave the puffins alone if you promise to leave me alone. I don't want anyone to know I'm here."

"What about me? I know."

"Anyone that might interfere with what I'm doing here."

"I already interfered."

"Yeah, well. Okay?"

"I guess. Okay."

He turned to go. He hadn't answered her about the gull eggs.

"Are you set for food?" she called after him.

"Yup," he answered. "I'm going to make me a fire and steam some clams." He pulled his jacket close around him.

"You want any cookies or anything?"

"No," he lied. "I'm living off the land." He had to get away from her before she heard his empty stomach protest.

13

It was almost too good to be true. Almost, because, from what Joellen could see, he wasn't anything to look at. That didn't matter, though. His showing up out of the blue—or out of the gray—gave her a fresh direction for her story. It would take awhile to figure out how a stranger fitted in. But at least she had something new to work with. Not only was there abandonment and maybe a murder or else the discovery of some crime or treasure long hidden in the recesses of that underground passage, but now there was a stranger who played some crucial role in all this.

She unrolled her sleeping bag, set out the small lantern, and sat down with her notebook. "She wasted no time looking around for food. She had no idea how long she would be on her own. First she picked raspberries. They were very good, but not filling. So she went to the part of the island where there were clams." Orcutt Cove?

Joellen paused. Would the girl take her long skirt off or

tie it up somehow? Or would she just let it get all wet and muddy? Joellen gave this some thought. She herself preferred shorts to rolled-up jeans, which usually got mucky anyway. Besides, how could anyone dig clams while holding a skirt? "She took the ribbon that tied back her hair and used it to hitch her skirt up around her waist. She left her shoes and socks on a rock above the high-water mark. Then she went to look for airholes in the muddy sand. It was hard because her hair got all over her face. It was the style then for girls and women to let their hair grow very long, and hers was a mess of curls that never looked neat." Joellen's hand rose to her own head, felt the kerchief that confined her own mess of curls, and went on writing. "Also, when she cleared away the mud, the clams squirted up at her. In spite of all this trouble, she soon had enough clams for a good meal."

Joellen tried to picture what the girl would do with those clams. If she had matches, they would probably be wet and ruined. Besides, maybe matches weren't even invented yet. So how would she build a fire? Even if she were hungry enough to eat clams raw, how would she pry open the shells?

At this point, if Joellen had been at home, she would probably have yelled for help. Mom never minded being interrupted for a good reason, even when she was working. She might not provide an answer to Joellen's question, but she would suggest where to look for information.

"The girl was weak with hunger and all that she had suffered when she struggled out of the freezing water. She had used up most of her energy looking for the others. Now she needed the food she had found. She carried the clams in her skirt and dumped them in a heap while she put on her shoes and socks. It was a lucky thing that clams had no feet to walk away on, because the tide was coming in

66

and there would be no more digging for another twelve hours."

Joellen left the notebook open, the pencil beside it. Taken at a glance, all that writing looked good, but not enough was happening, and she had contradicted what she had written before. If the girl had seen the others drown, why would she have used up energy looking for them?

Joellen added a note to herself to fix this. Was it time for the stranger to show up with fire? Was he good or evil? If she were home now, she might ask Mom to read what she had written. But Mom might tell her that it was too soon for feedback. Mom didn't like to comment on Joellen's projects until they were done.

Leaning back, she listened to the mournful foghorn. Now that the birds had quieted down, it came right through the stone like an eerie call from some creature of the deep. There was no point trying to use that sound in her story to create atmosphere since there wouldn't have been a horn way back then. It was even hard to write about hunger after shoveling in all that stew she'd had for supper tonight.

She wasn't ready to go to sleep either. She could always explore the underground passage a bit. But even with spare flashlight batteries, Joellen didn't feel like going there alone. Abbie might do it tomorrow. She would be better company than no one.

Joellen closed her eyes. She imagined footsteps approaching. Imagined? Her eyes shot open. There were footsteps, real ones. Scrambling up, she dashed to the tower stairs and climbed until she had gone around the curve.

She didn't think it would be anyone but the boy. But why had he come back here? What about his fire, his mess of clams?

Mounting the cellar stairs, he called out, "Hey, are you here?"

She shrank against the wall. Maybe if he didn't find her, he'd go away again.

"Where are you?" he said, arriving at the doorway. "I'm coming in." But he stopped. Not that he needed to, he told himself, taking note of the battery lamp lighting the room and the cartons marked "PUFFIN PROJECT." She had taken over this place like she had a right to it. He had even more of a right, since his ancestor had been lightkeeper in this very building. Not that he intended to bring up an ancestor who was the only keeper on the Maine coast to desert his lighthouse.

Where was that girl anyway? Why didn't she answer him?

He walked over to her things, his glance first falling on a candy bar tossed carelessly on top of the sleeping bag. He gulped air. He had to clench his fists to keep from snatching up the candy and ripping off the paper. He made his eyes focus elsewhere and found himself reading a description of someone whose image he might have glimpsed in the fogged mirror.

He dropped to his knees. Hadn't he convinced himself that the reflection had been an illusion? Yet here it was, tangled locks concealing the features, a figure out of Grandad's world of family ruin and wrongs never righted.

Joellen didn't like the way everything had gone still. What was that guy up to? Quietly, pausing after each step, she made her way down to a point where he came into view, bent over her sleeping bag. She shrank back. Definitely weird, she thought.

Chris sat back on his heels. It was just sinking in that this notebook mentioned stuff that could have come right out of Grandad's mouth. Chris turned back a page to read more.

Hearing the page turn, Joellen realized that he had her notebook. Springing to the floor, she landed with a thud and a yell. When he dropped the notebook, she dived for it.

"Who do you think you are, sneaking in here and looking at my things?" she railed at him.

"Well, why didn't you answer me? I wasn't sneaking."

"You just keep your hands and your eyes off my things," she ordered.

"Who made you queen of the lighthouse?" he demanded.

His question was distracting. It trimmed the sharp edge from her anger. "Queen of the lighthouse," she repeated musingly. It had a good ring. She wondered if she could make a title like that fit her story.

Chris sensed that they were on different ground now. He spoke quickly, just in case the ground shifted under them again and she remembered that she was ticked off. "I came back," he explained, "because I forgot something important." He told her about the sheep trapped in the pit. Maybe together they could get her out.

Joellen nodded. The guy actually sounded as if he knew what he was talking about. "You want me to get my dad?"

Chris shook his head. "Only if we can't do it. I'm not supposed to have anything to do with people while I'm here. I could use some extra rope, though."

"There's potwarp down in the cellar."

"Worth trying," he said.

"Now?" she asked.

"No," he answered, "first light. Before your dad comes back."

"Will the sheep be all right overnight?"

"She has to be. I was hauling feed to her for hours today. Turns out she likes kelp better than rockweed."

Joellen was impressed that he had come all the way back in the dark to rescue the sheep. He couldn't have had much time to get a fire going and cook his clams. "Did you eat?" she asked him.

He shrugged. "I'll make up for it tomorrow."

She picked up her knapsack and dumped out a spare flashlight, a banana, a package of cookies, a tube of toothpaste, and a second candy bar. "Help yourself," she said.

"No, thanks," he told her.

"Aren't you hungry?"

He grinned. "Enough to eat the toothpaste, tube and all. But it's against the rules. It's hard to explain."

"I know, you told me. You have to live off the land. I hope you get something worthwhile for what you're going through."

He rubbed his eyes. At the moment it seemed so senseless that only his stubbornness kept him from breaking down and gobbling up everything in sight. He headed for the stairs to the cellar. In the doorway he turned. "I'm Chris Fossett," he said.

"I'm Joellen Roth."

"Joellen," he repeated in a way that was almost a question.

She was used to that. She said, "Part of my father's name and my mother's all in one. I guess they knew I'd be the only kid." Annoyed at herself for telling him more than he had asked, she watched him turn and leave.

It was only after she was snug in her sleeping bag that she wondered how he would get all the way back across the island in the dark.

14

He awoke cramped with cold. It was not yet light, but there was a gray cast to the eastern sky. Today it would clear.

He shook off the branches he had used as a cover. Spending the night in the corner of the old foundation had been smelly but fairly protected. Maybe the year's collection of sheep droppings generated some heat; at least it had served as insulation.

On his way into the lighthouse he brushed himself off. He guessed he was still pretty sheepy. Never mind, he thought as he called through the bulkhead to wake the girl, by the time they were finished she'd probably stink, too.

Joellen sprang up. "Coming," she shouted. But she

stopped to leave a note telling her father she had gone for a walk.

"Hurry," he told her. "We'll need your knapsack empty. And bring the potwarp."

By the time they left the open headland, the sky had lightened, the sea had gone from dull gray to slate blue.

It was slow work getting through the brambles, then even slower as they made their way into the alder thicket.

"I'm stopping," she called to him.

"Something wrong?"

"I have to pee, if you must know."

He waited without comment.

"Okay," she finally told him.

A couple of years ago Chris and his father had been able to cut across the island on this path. Now it was so overgrown Chris thought of turning back and taking the coast route past Dread Mans Cove. But he was worried about the time. If they could get through this way, they would reach the spruce woods much more quickly. Afterward, after the sheep had been freed, they could take their time, and Chris could make sure that Joellen kept clear of the danger spots.

The last ten or fifteen minutes were brutal, though. A lot of young growth blocked the path. Clearly the sheep weren't keeping up with the spruce. Either they had plenty of grass or their numbers were way down. He would be sure to mention this to Dad.

The farther in they went, the more Joellen began to wonder whether Chris was on the level. Why was he leading her into this mess? It was almost impossible to take more than a step upright. Branches became cruel hands reaching out to trip her, to snag her, to force her to her knees.

"You all right?" he called back to her when she fell behind.

"Yup," she shouted. Whatever he was up to, she wasn't about to let him know how tough this was for her.

It occurred to him that even after they got to the sheep, Joellen might not be strong enough to make a difference. If they couldn't free the sheep together, he supposed he would have to give in and ask her father for help. If that happened, would it mean that the contest was over? Maybe not, maybe only if he ate their food. Think of it, real food. No, thinking of it was dangerous. It made his knees go weak.

Joellen was the first to hear the ewe blat. She called to Chris, who doubled back on the nonpath.

"Are you sure?" he asked her. "It might've been some other sheep calling the others."

"Of course it might've," she snapped. "I don't know your sheep, and this one didn't introduce itself. I heard it, that's all."

They waited a moment. The sheep blatted again.

"Huh," Chris said. "I guess we overshot. It must be her. You stay here," he told Joellen. He worked his way up a rise, climbed a blowdown, and gazed all around. Nothing looked the same from here, nothing. So he went on, closing in on the approximate location of the sheep they had heard. All at once he noticed broken spruce branches. He had ripped them off to feed the ewe.

"Okay!" he shouted back over his shoulder. "Come on this way."

"This way," Joellen grumbled to herself. "Like he's turned a corner and there's a sign to show me where.

"Chris," she called after stumbling on another fifty yards or so.

"Here," he answered. "You're too far west."

West meant nothing to her. "I forgot my compass," she retorted.

"Too far to the right," he told her. "I was doing that, too," he said as she finally caught sight of the immense oak and then of him. "I guess that's why we overshot. I kept heading west."

They looked down at the ewe and lamb. He braced himself, expecting Joellen to gush about the adorable baby. He'd better not be rude.

But all she said was "The sheep must be awfully hungry." She pointed into the pit at the branches, which were stripped clean. "Should we feed her before we try to get her out?"

Chris had to admit it wasn't a bad idea. But he was worried about his own food supply. He needed time to get clams and mussels while the tide was out. "Let's just see what we can do first," he said. As he fastened the rope around a protruding root, he showed Joellen where to loop the rope whenever there was enough slack.

Together they straightened the potwarp, which was so stiff it seemed almost brittle.

Then he slid into the pit with it. The ewe leaped away, nearly trampling her lamb. Chris snatched it out from under her and handed it up to Joellen. "Into the knapsack," he directed.

Joellen had to stretch out on her stomach to take the lamb from Chris. It was surprisingly strong. It flailed, all legs. Joellen was terrified of breaking one of them while she folded them enough to shove the lamb inside her knapsack. As she struggled, she was vaguely aware of a more violent struggle in progress in the pit. By the time she had the lamb secured, with only its head emerging, Chris had the ewe down, bawling for her lamb, but not yet tied.

"I can't . . . yet," he panted. "I need another hand."

Joellen slid down to him. The ewe lurched, trying to thrust herself free. Chris, who was sprawled with the ewe against him, twisted her head.

"Don't," Joellen told him. "You're hurting her."

Chris, one ear ringing from where he had been kicked, said, "Don't tell me how to handle sheep."

"Well, I won't help you if you hurt her."

"Listen, will you? I'm trying to save the damn sheep's life. Now get the potwarp all the way around her. Farther forward," he yelled as the ewe flung herself out of his grasp. "Damn!" he shouted, tackling her again and throwing her onto her rump. "Now, here," he told Joellen. He was able to knot the potwarp after she pulled it around the ewe's body just behind the forelegs. "Quick," he said. "Hand over the line, then get back up there. You've got to be ready to take up the slack."

Climbing up was harder than Joellen had imagined. As the loosened subsoil that formed the wall of the pit crumbled away, she understood how the sheep had become trapped.

"Step on my shoulder," Chris told her. "Go on. Hurry. We've got to get moving here." It was the lift she needed to haul herself up and out.

She watched as Chris positioned himself behind the ewe. Then he shoved. But the frantic ewe, thinking her lamb was behind her, resisted with all her strength.

Joellen dragged the knapsack to the edge of the pit. Fortunately the lamb bleated. The ewe lunged toward it, giving Chris a chance to thrust her upward. But Joellen was too late to get the rope snubbed around the root. Chris swore. Joellen said it wasn't her fault. He said he hadn't said it was. The ewe bawled and the lamb wailed. This time when the ewe tried to clamber up to it and Chris thrust from behind, Joellen whipped the loose line twice around.

By now Chris was grunting so hard that he couldn't speak. His eyes were full of dirt and his mouth was full of wool. He was pushing the ewe with his head, shoulders, and arms.

Joellen managed to make one more loop around the root. At this point the ewe was almost hanging there, her hind legs kicking so hard that Chris had to break away. Quickly he clambered up and out and grabbed the taut line. He pulled. Joellen knelt at the edge of the pit, reached down, and grabbed the ewe's head behind the ears. Slowly the sheep inched upward, her legs dragging under her, until finally Joellen was able to grab first one foreleg and then the other.

Suddenly with a tremendous burst of power, the ewe's upper body cleared the edge of the pit. Chris leaned over, grabbing fistfuls of wool to keep her coming. He just barely rolled out of the way as she lumbered over the top.

In an instant she was on her feet. But when she tried to bound away, she was checked by the line.

"Show her the lamb," Chris gasped. "Don't let it loose yet."

The ewe didn't recognize the head sticking out of the knapsack. Chris was scared. Only now did it occur to him that under stress the ewe might reject her lamb.

He went over to Joellen and unzipped the knapsack. The lamb struggled as he lifted it out and held it upright so its mother could see all of it. For one moment she seemed beyond caring. Then the lamb bleated softly, and the ewe's mothering instinct was restored.

Chris heaved a sigh. He still had to get the potwarp off

her. Holding the lamb in front, he approached the ewe. She started to back, so he took the lamb away from her again. She followed, almost to the stump. Then, in what amounted to a single gesture, he offered her the lamb and tackled her, bringing her thumping to the ground.

Joellen snatched up the lamb to keep it out of kicking range. In the next instant the ewe sprang up, the potwarp trailing but no longer attached. By now the lamb was nosing around and bumping at Joellen's legs. It seemed to have chosen a gentler mother than its own. When the ewe uttered a low, insistent command and Joellen turned the lamb around, it finally responded. As soon as it skittered over to its real mother, the ewe retreated. Then she stopped to let it nurse.

Chris and Joellen sat on the rope-strewn ground and grinned. They sat there grinning until the lamb came out from beneath the udder and began to poke around the ewe's front end. At this point the ewe grabbed a mouthful of spruce needles. Then it seemed to dawn on her that she was truly free. Casting a final glare at Chris and Joellen, she led her lamb away.

15

"I better get you back," he said finally.

She bristled. "I can get back on my own. Just point me right."

"We'll follow the shoreline. It's easier. But there's a tricky bit. I'll see you past that."

He didn't get it. She didn't need to be conducted around an island. She said, "Anyway, I'm in no hurry."

"Well, I am. I need to beat the tide. I'm going to dig me a whole mess of clams."

Joellen straightened. "Where?" When she had wondered where the girl in her story would find clams, she had recalled his mentioning Orcutt Cove.

"I'll show you," he said, "if you're sure you're not in a hurry."

They got up. She shook out her knapsack, remembered

the candy in the small pocket, and offered him some. He shook his head as he coiled the rope and then the stiff potwarp. But when she tore off the wrapping, the aroma of chocolate hit him in the pit of his stomach. A small groan escaped him.

"What?" she asked, her mouth full. She stared into the empty pit.

Chris couldn't take his eyes off her jaw as she chewed. It made him think of the ewe taking her first bite of food on her own. Not a flattering comparison, but that's what happened with food on his brain.

Joellen said, "Don't we have to fill this hole up or something so another sheep doesn't get stuck in it?"

"Yeah," he answered. "I've already thought of that." It was a lie. But so what? "I've got some drift junk I can throw in there. It'll take awhile to fill it up, but I don't have anything else to do except dig clams and pick mussels."

She looked him up and down as if measuring him.

He couldn't keep from defending his being there. "Nobody has to understand," he told her. "I won't try to explain."

She shrugged, letting him know that she wasn't even curious.

He mustn't let her get to him. After all, she had really helped him with the sheep. So he said, "Come on, I'll show you the mudflats. You can even have some breakfast clams." After gathering up the rope and potwarp, he led her on across the island.

It was easier to keep up with him now. For one thing he had cleared a path between the beach and the pit. Joellen still had to vault over or scramble under fallen trees, but she didn't have to fight any dense, brambly undergrowth.

When they came out of the woods, the outlook was utterly unlike the steep headland on the lighthouse end of the island. Here, where the spruce woods ended, the ground gave way to a small stony beach that sloped gradually toward outlying boulders. Beyond these huge, rounded rocks, their contours softened by masses of rockweed, black lumps lay nearly covered by water. One of them moved, and what had looked like the tip of a ledge became a seal. It raised its head, stared shoreward a moment, then slid beneath the surface.

"Tide's turned," Chris said. Down on the beach he collected his clamming equipment, the top of a wooden lobster crate, the rusted section of barrel stave he had already used for digging, and a few metal parts of a trawler door. "Diggers," he told Joellen. "I'll dig and you pick up." He handed her some plastic netting he had tied to make a crude sack.

Looking at all the stones on the beach, she was glad to leave the digging to him. But then it turned out that this was only where he had made camp. The clams were beyond a long sloping rock that divided the area below his camp from an open stretch of gravelly mud full of airholes.

It didn't take long to fill the net sack. Chris dragged it into the water to wash the clams, then emptied them onto the lobster crate cover, which he had strewn with rockweed. He left her to fill the bag again while he carried the first haul of clams back to camp and started a fire.

When she had the sack full, she pushed up her jeans and carried it into the shallows. But her own steps stirred up the mud and sand. She had to go farther out to get the clams clean. She was soaked to the waist, but she was determined to get the job done on her own. By the time she staggered onto dry land her legs and feet were numb.

She saw smoke rising toward the trees. It propelled her

80

back to the camp. Chris was down by the boulders picking armfuls of rockweed. She stood upwind but close to the fire. Her legs began to tingle and then sting as the feeling came into them.

Chris dumped his load of rockweed and started back for more. He didn't ask her to help, and she didn't want to walk into that freezing water again, but she could tell that he was aware of what she did and didn't do. She waited until his back was to her, and then she ran to another boulder some distance from him and began to tear the weed from the rock. So far so good. She wasn't wading yet. But her pant legs were cold and stiff against her skin. When she hurried back to dump her armful of weed, she stole another minute beside the fire.

But as soon as she caught sight of Chris returning, she ran back to her boulder and loaded up with more rockweed.

By the time she joined Chris he had doused the fire with rockweed and was dropping clams on top. After he had covered the clams with more weed, he carried the full sack above the tide line, spread rockweed over and around it, and then set stones on the entire heap.

Joellen drew as close to the smoldering fire as she could. At first it simply sputtered and sizzled beneath the rockweed. But soon a delicious clam smell came steaming out. Chris came back with a forked branch and lifted off a layer of rockweed. Some of the clams had opened, but he covered them anyway until the whole batch was done.

It didn't take long. He made a kind of pot holder out of fresh rockweed and picked out the steamed clams before putting on more to cook. A flat board was their table. Chris didn't speak a word until he had eaten all the clams except the few that Joellen took for herself.

She couldn't help thinking how much better they would

taste dipped in melted butter, but they were sweet, if gritty, and by the time the next batch was ready, so was she.

Finally he heaved a sigh and said, "I bet that old ewe feels like this by now, too."

"How can you tell she's old?" Joellen asked him.

"Tag number," he said.

"What?"

"Ear tag. All the sheep on this island are my dad's. He keeps track of them with the tags. She's number 212."

Why hadn't Chris mentioned that the sheep belonged to his father? "Why does your father keep them here?" she asked.

"Lots of reasons," he answered. "Sheep have been grazing some of these islands for hundreds of years. My dad manages flocks on four others beside this one. Without the sheep, most of the islands would be dense woods and nothing else."

She said, "My father must've spoken to yours then, because he tried to get them off this one, on account of the puffins."

Chris nodded. "That's where I heard the name. You know, the sheep don't bother the birds any."

"I think it has to do with the burrows. Sometimes the sheep eat away the grass roots and then the turf caves in." She thought about mentioning the terns.

"Whatever," Chris replied. He didn't feel like getting into an argument with her. "Anyway," he went on, "the sheep are safer out on these islands than on the mainland."

"Except when they get stuck," Joellen pointed out.

"That's true. But they don't get chased and killed by dogs or coyotes. Of course a few get shot every winter. There are some people around who think anything out here's free for the taking. We expect that now."

"That's disgusting," Joellen declared.

Chris shrugged. He was on the edge of telling her what it was like to round up the island sheep every fall and carry off the lambs to market.

"So how many sheep does your father take care of?" she asked.

"Maybe three hundred," he said, "give or take."

"Are you going to do that, too?"

"Not me," he blurted. "No way."

"How come?" she pressed. "What do you want to do instead?"

He leaned back, his arms behind his head, and felt the sun on his face. "I only know what I don't want to do," he told her finally. "I don't want to tie up lambs and stack them like herring for the smokehouse. I don't want to leave all those ewes climbing around the rocks bawling to their lambs that are out in the boat hollering." He had never spoken about these feelings before. He couldn't believe that he was spilling his guts to a stranger, a girl, a kid who had to be at least three years younger than he was. "What about you?" he said, trying to turn the conversation around. "You going to do birds?"

Joellen shook her head. "I'm going to be a writer," she said.

"What, like for TV? Movies?" Then before she could answer, he remembered the story in her notebook. He had skimmed only a page or so before she stopped him.

She was replying now. He had missed her first words. She was saying, "And I need to find out more history. You know, like what people needed for living on an island like this, for instance, before TV and loran and all. What their clothes felt like, and their shoes. Stuff like that."

He sat up and poked around in the embers. Man, he thought, he could do with a few hot dogs now to round off the clams. He said, lazily, "You should talk to my grandfather sometime. He knows a lot." Chris paused. "And if he doesn't know it, he'll make it up. When I was a little kid, he used to fill me full of all kinds of crap. Anyway, he has old things in his house on Spars Island."

Joellen leaned toward him. "Like what?" she prompted. "From when?"

Chris thought a moment. There were old tools in with new ones, some pictures, household stuff. But they were all mixed together, and he had no idea when they were made. Then he remembered the schoolbook. When he stayed for any length of time on Spars Island, out of sheer boredom he would read it over and over. Every story in it had a moral, either about being kind to animals or obedient to parents. The kids in it bore no resemblance to anyone he knew. He said, "There's this old-fashioned book. With an ad on the back for a Cheap Book Store."

Joellen laughed. "Where was it, this bookstore?"

"Boston, I think. The book was called *Easy Reading Lessons*. It had a date, 1843, something like that. Grandad said he had learned to read with this book, and for a while I thought that meant he was a kid in 1843." Chris grinned. "Till one day I did a little figuring. The book was already an antique when Grandad was a kid. When I asked him about it, he said it was his grandmother's. Some kid drew in it, too. I could never figure out what the pictures were about."

Pictures, thought Joellen, were just what she needed. Maybe they would show people wearing whatever people wore in 1843. "Does he still have it?" she asked.

"I guess. I don't know. People from away come to old-timers like him and try to buy stuff off them. He doesn't like strangers poking around, so he doesn't do business with them. But he's given my aunt a few things for her shop."

Chris scowled, trying to recover in his mind's eye the curious house some long-ago child had drawn, the ship full of skinny boxes like coffins with stick figures in them. Grandad said that his grandmother had once told him the pictures were drawn by the island girl, but Grandad stressed that it was easy for his grandmother to blame someone who wasn't there to speak for herself. For that matter, Chris now realized, Grandad's grandmother had placed the blame on someone who wasn't there, period.

"One lesson was called 'How Books Are Made,'" Chris told Joellen. "It was all about making paper from rags, about writing and printing and binding, and stuff. I think my grandfather suspected that way back when she was young, his grandmother had gone at that book with a pencil and didn't want to admit it when she was grown up and teaching him to read from it. Grandad's grandmother, or whoever the kid was, couldn't have thought much of the lesson's moral, which was that after all those things and people and work, we should treat books with care and keep them clean and nice."

Childish drawings of a cow and sheep and people filled the top and bottom margins of this lesson. "Someone marked up that page something terrible," he went on. "It's hard to believe it could've been Grandad's grandmother, though, because she raised him and made him learn from that book."

"That doesn't mean that she wasn't a brat when she was little," Joellen said.

Chris stretched and rose. "I suppose. I just can't picture someone like Grandad or a person even older than him ever being, you know, like me." He kicked at the embers. Satisfied that the fire was out, he said that they'd better get going. He wanted that hole filled in by the end of the day.

16

Joellen leaned over her notebook to shade the page. She could have moved closer to the lighthouse, but then she'd be cold. Besides, she wanted her father to see her carrying on normally. He had fumed and scolded and threatened to ground her until she had pointed out that she was already grounded on the island and trying to make the best of it. Then his tone had changed. He had been worried, he said. If she went off on her own, she should check back more often. He left it at that.

He didn't used to be like this. He hadn't the slightest inkling of how she felt being scolded like a little kid within earshot of his girlfriend.

Joellen wrote furiously. Thanks to the fight with Dad, suddenly her story had momentum. And a clear direction.

The girl had to have been deliberately abandoned, even if she didn't realize it yet. Joellen couldn't wait to describe the girl's feelings when she learned the truth.

But first the girl must discover a buried treasure. The underground passage had seemed the ideal place for something to have been concealed, but that was before Joellen had seen the huge crater left by the uprooted oak tree. Could the girl come across something exposed when a huge tree was toppled in the storm that caused the shipwreck?

Joellen paused, squinting out on the bird cliff. Two puffins marched over the rock face, their brilliant beaks displaying heads and tails of small fish. Dad and Abbie were down there somewhere trying to complete the puffin census. Shading the page with her hand, Joellen pondered the treasure she had just invented. What should it be? What could it be? She still didn't know the name of the girl who was about to find it. She only knew that the girl was recovering from the ordeal of a shipwreck and no longer dazed. The treasure might be a weapon or money or a clue to some sort of mystery, maybe a crime. Did it have anything to do with pirates?

Joellen jotted down all the place-names that might provide a lead: Dread Mans Cove, Folly Point, and, farther off, Parsons Sham and Sham Rock. *Sham* meant "phony," didn't it? Was the treasure a sham? No, better than that, it would be proof of a sham, some crooked deal, a fraud. Was there an underworld in olden times? A mob? Well, there were pirates. There must have been other kinds of criminals as well. Did she really want her solitary girl involved with those types? But what if just by accident she had witnessed a crime? Maybe that was it. Maybe there was a conflict between her longing for rescue and the possibility that her rescuer might be out to get her.

Joellen shivered. Even with the sun on her shoulders, the wind had a bite to it. But she kept on writing now that the story was taking shape. Later she would go back over earlier pages and cross out false leads.

When Dad and Abbie appeared declaring that it was past lunchtime, she was ready to put the story aside for a while.

Earlier, after Dad's tirade, Abbie had offered breakfast, so of course Joellen had insisted she didn't want any. Now she didn't bother to disguise her hunger. Before Abbie had finished cutting the cheese, Joellen had devoured two slices of bread with gobs of peanut butter and was looking around for a second course.

Dad and Abbie were talking about their findings. So far they had verified that eleven of the puffins that had been artificially reared and fledged from here were now tending eggs. Dad was slightly discouraged, Abbie trying to put a good spin on the count.

"They could be late, that's all. This is their first year, and they may not be in sync with the native puffins."

Dad nodded. "In March there were so many in the water around here I was sure more would breed and be laying by now."

"But we've just seen some doing courtship displays."

"Courtship or aggression," he said. "By the time the later eggs hatch, there'll be less protection from the gulls."

"How come?" asked Joellen, forgetting for a moment to stay remote and sullen.

"When they first come from the sea, they wait for more and more to arrive before taking to the burrows. It's the same deal when they're feeding their young. They swim close with their beaks full and then wait for more before flying up and landing. On Machias Seal Island I've seen them fly to land in such overwhelming numbers that the gulls don't get much chance to steal away the fish they're bringing to the burrows."

"What would happen to, say, the last puffin?" she asked him. "If it's late. Would it be killed?"

"Not necessarily. But its young wouldn't stand much of a chance."

Joellen mulled this over. The last puffin would be like the girl in her story, abandoned by its kind, left to its own devices. If the mirrors were still here, it might gaze longingly at its own reflection so as not to feel so alone. But of course there would be no mirror in the time of her story. So if someone showed up, the girl would be drawn to him simply because he was a fellow human being. This could be dangerous. How could she protect herself against such a predator, a human gull?

"Anything wrong?" Dad asked.

Joellen came back from her story. She shook her head. Then another question formed in her mind, and she spoke. "If predators aren't bad because they're part of the natural world and they're just keeping themselves alive, then what about people that prey on other people?"

"You mean like muggers and robbers?"

She shrugged. "And others going after people that are weak or helpless or just happen to be in the wrong place. No one says it's all right to stalk or hurt someone because it's natural." She knew that if she tried to talk about a great black-backed gull slaughtering a chick, he wouldn't get it because he'd be so intent on declaring his position. "If you see a crime," she said, almost pleading with him to see what she saw, "aren't you supposed to stop it or report it?"

"Right," Dad agreed. "But human nature is another thing. So is human behavior. Society makes it more complicated than blackbacks and herring gulls."

"Don't forget," put in Abbie, "that puffins are predators, too. They prey on fish."

Did that mean that any person or animal that protected itself and its young might also be a predator? Joellen shook her head. "Are you saying that everyone hits on someone else?" she asked.

"No!" Dad and Abbie exclaimed together.

Joellen couldn't bear their united stand. They seemed so clear about everything that put her in a muddle. She grabbed her jacket.

"Where are you going?" Dad demanded.

If he had asked in an easier tone, she might have told him about Chris. But she retorted, "Where do you think? I'm on an island, aren't I?"

"Be back by six," he told her.

She responded with the slightest nod she could manage and headed for the alder thicket. Once she was out of sight, she would bear off toward Dread Mans Cove.

17

After seeing Joellen safely past Dread Mans Cove, Chris had retraced their path until he came abreast of Folly Point. There he stopped to cast his eye out over the sheep spread across the gentle headland. There was no way to distinguish number 212 from any of the other ewes cropping the close grass out there. Lambs ran from rock to rock, always seeking the highest spot from which to leap and tear around the grazing mothers. One of them must be the freed lamb. How did it feel to find that its world had opened up and was full of space and light and other lambs?

He had meant to turn into the woods and go straight to work filling the pit. Instead he stretched out on the moss-covered turf at the edge of the trees and let the sun finish the drying process the fire had begun. He drowsed, started awake, and drowsed some more.

Later when he looked out over Folly Point, there wasn't a sheep in sight. He supposed they had retreated to the woods. Maybe a lobsterman had come by. They were wary of boats, especially the ones that hovered offshore. The sheep had no way to tell the difference between men who pulled traps and men who stopped to load rifles or shotguns.

With this thought, his shepherding instincts kicked in. He still had the pit to take care of before another sheep got itself trapped.

He decided to head straight into the woods. He was getting more familiar with the lay of the land, so he didn't think he'd have any trouble finding the downed oak.

But he had to detour so often that he kept losing his bearings. He took any direction that looked like a sheep path until he realized it was leading him out of the woods. By the time he figured he was nearing the area, he could hear branches break and other sounds that made him think of a sheep thrashing in panic. Another one caught? Damn.

He tried to run, stumbled over a root, and pitched headlong onto a thistle. A thistle? What was a thistle doing in the woods? They grew in the open where the sun could reach them. He swore to himself as he pulled broken thistle spines from the front and sleeves of his shirt. One side of his face was scratched open. Nothing serious, but it stung, and the stinging was a reminder of how dumb he had been to try to run here.

He was walking with his hand across the rawness of his cheek and over one eye when something in front of him shifted. For a second he had the sensation of the ground rolling away from him. Then he lunged for whatever was moving and felt it jerked out from under him.

"What the hell—?" he started to exclaim.

"Chris?" Joellen responded.

He stopped. "Oh, it's you," he said, stepping through the trees and around a lichen-covered boulder to find her dragging a broadly branched young spruce. "What do you think you're doing pulling up more trees?" he demanded. And what was she doing here ahead of him? He felt like a fool.

"With some, it's easier than breaking branches. See, the roots aren't very deep. It's amazing they've even grown this much. Anyway, I'm getting this stuff for the hole." She knew she was rattling on too much, but it kept her from blurting something else.

At first she had just been surprised to discover that he hadn't returned to the pit. Then she had begun to think of all the possible accidents. Hadn't he just shown her where one false step on unsupported turf could land you on the rocks at the bottom of Dread Mans Cove? What she wanted to do now was yell at him. On the tip of her tongue were the very indignant phrases her father had used to berate her. "I guess we better make a kind of platform," she babbled on. "You know, like supports first and then something across." She dropped the tip of the spruce, faced him, and saw blood. "So you did have an accident," she declared.

"What?" he retorted. "Oh, this. It isn't anything." He wasn't about to give her the satisfaction of letting her know that he had embraced a thistle.

"So what happened?" she insisted. "Where were you?"

"Busy, as it happens." Why didn't she just buzz off? "I wasn't expecting you," he added, sounding as stiff and formal as some rich dude on television. If he had just told her the simple truth, it would already be over and forgotten.

"Well, it looks gross," she told him. She went back to dragging the tree.

94

Chris stood there a moment. In spite of his irritation, he found himself grinning at her reaction. So what if she had a head start on him? He could catch up in no time. He swung around and pulled back one of the oak limbs until it snapped.

"If you strip that," she told him when he finally brought it around to the edge of the pit, "we can use it for one of the crosspieces. You know," she added into his silence, "like ceiling beams."

She had it all figured out. His father was right about those bird people. Like everyone from away, you couldn't tell them anything. "You're the expert," Chris said.

It didn't take him long to turn sour, she thought. Well, he could fix the pit any old way he liked. She stomped off in search of another shallow-rooted spruce.

He looked over the situation. She had actually collected quite a heap of brush and branches. She had even organized them according to size and type. Of course she was right about the pit. It should be crisscrossed with stuff, beginning with straight pieces strong enough to bear the weight of everything else they added to build up to ground level.

She kept on hauling small trees and branches until she had worked the disappointment out of her system. Eventually it occurred to her that his sour disposition might have something to do with his boring diet. She had devoured bread and peanut butter and cheese, and that was after a candy bar beforehand and some of his clams later on. Still, he could have accepted the food she offered. That was his choice.

She stole a glance at him as he cleaned off another straight limb. He was kind of skinny. He couldn't be anorexic, could he? Why would someone starve himself on purpose? He had said it was some kind of test. Or was it a contest? Either way, it was weird. She supposed he might be mad now because he had turned down real food. She had already polished off the banana, but she did have an apple in her pocket. She would gladly hand it over to him if it would help him to act human again.

She said, "If you found an apple out here, could you eat it?"

He stopped, his hand reaching up to his bloody cheek and then quickly dropping back to the wood. "Sure. Just the way I'd eat beach peas, if there were any, or raspberries or blackberries. Anything natural," he added, "anything found." He paused. "Like an egg."

She knew he was needling her. Her older cousin used to do it, too. She had enough experience not to react. Instead she pulled the apple from her pocket and placed it with obvious deliberation at the edge of the pit.

Chris didn't budge. It would be cheating to take it. He had to hold out against temptation. "Thanks anyway," he told her.

"So go ahead," she urged.

He shook his head. "If apples did grow here, they wouldn't be fruit till late summer."

He was beyond stubborn. Not a very useful model for either the hero or the outlaw in her story. She picked up the apple and returned it to her pocket.

They went back to work. When Chris had cleaned off branches from green trunks long enough to span the pit, he jumped down inside to inspect the prospects. Joellen knelt at the edge.

"Can you gouge out holes to stick the poles into?" she asked.

"I can try. But the sides crumbled when the sheep tried to climb out."

"Too bad we don't have a spade."

"Or a drill. What've we got for a digger?"

Joellen rummaged through the piles and came up with a twisted root branch and a flat stone. He tried them both, then ended up using his bare hands. At the opposite side of the pit he made another hole facing the first one.

"It's not deep enough," Joellen said.

"Better shallow than loose," he told her. "Let's try a tree."

She held the bottom while he broke off the top. Leaning on the middle until it bowed, he slid his end into one hole while she forced the other into the hole across from it. He gave it a gingerly tug. It stayed put.

The next hole was harder to keep small. He had to move farther over, and still the subsoil crumbled.

"Try it anyway," she suggested. "Maybe it won't matter."

He looked doubtful. "It ought to be a tight fit."

"So wedge it," she said. "After you've got the pole in."

It nettled him that he hadn't thought of it himself. "That might work," he admitted.

When they had the next pole lodged in place, she presented him with an assortment of sticks to use as wedges. But he needed something flatter. Like the digger, only wider, so that it would act like a kind of shelf support for the tip of the pole. They pondered this a moment. Then his gaze fell on part of a stone protruding in the nonbearing wall below her. It had the look of a squared corner. He scraped subsoil away from around it until more was revealed.

"Not bad," he muttered.

"Perfect," she said.

Finally he was able to get a grip on it and pull. At first he couldn't get it unstuck. Then all of a sudden it gave way, along with a portion of gravelly dirt. He held it in both hands. "Maybe not," he said, scowling as he brushed off pebbles and sand. "I don't think it's stone after all."

"What is it, wood?" she asked, reaching out for it.

He didn't hand it over, but he showed it to her, an evenly shaped thing like a chunk of wood that might have been cut into a rectangle for a purpose. "It could work anyway," he said. "I mean, it doesn't feel rotten." He tapped it to prove his point.

Again she reached for it. This time he placed it in her hands. Her heart raced. It wasn't stone, and it didn't feel like wood. It reminded her of kelp found high above the tide line, kelp that had once grown tough and rubbery, attached to the ocean floor until it was torn from its roots by a violent storm and flung ashore. Whenever Joellen came across the dried-out fronds and long, twisted stems of kelp, they were hard to the touch, almost brittle. But what could have made this object so evenly shaped? She needed to clean it off some more, to get it out into the light for a good look.

"I'll find something else," she said, depositing the object beyond the stack of branches and on the far side of a standing tree.

She had practically snatched it from him. Taking charge again. It was a good thing she worked hard and had a brain. Otherwise he would have told her to get lost.

A short, forked branch she gave him did the trick, though it had to be broken to keep the pole from rolling.

Eventually he had to hike himself up and out to avoid being closed in by the last poles. These were harder to manage from above. Without Joellen at one end, he would never have got them in.

The rest was relatively easy. First the crosspieces were

laid, then branches, then more lengths. Later on his father would have to do something else to fill in the pit, but this covering would certainly do for the time being.

Joellen worked like a demon to quell the excitement that welled up in her. Excitement akin to alarm, because what she had written seemed to be coming true.

18

Satisfied with a job well done, Chris began to think about food. If he went down to the beach now and got a fire going, he could steam the rest of the clams and be on hand when the tide went down enough to pick a load of mussels before dark. He wasn't about to be caught again with nothing to eat. From now on he would stay at least one meal ahead.

He figured that if Joellen had found her way here alone, she could get herself back to the lighthouse without his help. Still, she had shared the work. He supposed he ought to share his clams.

He told her what he was about to do. "Coming?" he asked, not exactly an invitation.

Joellen shook her head. Either he had forgotten about

the object they had found or he didn't care that much. She waited for him to leave.

"I guess your dad needs you to help with the puffins," he said.

She shook her head again. She wished he'd just go, but she couldn't help answering him. "He doesn't need me. He has an assistant. Abbie. She used to be his student," Joellen added unnecessarily.

That brought Chris up short. Did it explain why Joellen didn't stay on the boat? "What's she like?" he asked.

Joellen shrugged. In spite of wanting Chris gone, she couldn't seem to cut him off. "I don't know. Pretty. Ask my father. He thinks she's perfect."

Chris realized he'd struck a nerve. Joellen, simmering, could explode in any direction. "What about your mother?" he asked, picking his words to sound neutral.

"What about her?" Joellen snapped. "She's a biologist, too. She's on a field trip of her own, it so happens. They're getting a divorce." Joellen's breath came short. Why couldn't she just shut up? It was none of his business. If she wasn't careful, she'd blurt out something really dumb about how love could make some people deaf and blind and forget who they were. "Have a nice clambake," she said pointedly.

Turning away, he realized that he was disappointed. It just went to show how desperate you could get for any kind of company when you were cut off from everyone else. When he glanced back, she was already gone. No, not gone. She was just farther over and not standing. He hoped she wasn't crying. He waited a moment. What was she up to?

Then he remembered the object she had snatched from him. "Joellen!" he shouted.

Startled, she rocked back on her heels. If only she had

waited another couple of minutes. "What?" she replied on a note of defiance.

He stomped toward her. "Let's see it," he said, reaching out.

Reluctantly she handed it to him. "I thought it might be a box," she said.

"Why?" he asked, turning it over and over in his hands. He scraped his nail across the flat surface. "It could almost be some kind of shell."

"What shell looks like a box?" she insisted.

He pulled out his knife, opened a blade, and scraped. Dirt flaked off. He pressed the blade harder.

"Careful," she warned.

"Why?" he said. "What can it hurt?"

She couldn't say that he might be destroying evidence. He already thought she was spacey imagining it a box.

"I think I'll take it downshore and clean it off in the water," he declared.

"No!" she cried. "You don't even know what it is."

"And you do?" he retorted. "Where do you get off telling me how to deal with my thing?"

"It's not just yours," she blurted. "It might be . . ." She faltered. He was giving her that disgusted look again. She could tell that all he wanted was to get rid of her. She had to make herself sound cool. "It could be something like a clue," she said, managing to keep her voice level. She could see that she had his attention now. "You know, like bones or made stuff someone left."

What did she mean? The sorts of things archaeologists dug up? He said, "I can't believe that anyone would bury a made thing in the middle of the woods. And if it's not made, washing it off can't hurt it."

She had to admit that made sense. But she wasn't about to let it go. "I thought you wanted to get your fire started," she reminded him.

He nodded. "And then I'll take care of this thing," he told her. Did she think he could be distracted that easily?

"I'll help with the firewood," she said.

"You're all heart," he replied grimly. But once they started off for the beach, he knew that in spite of her bossiness, he wasn't sorry to have her along.

She knew she'd better watch her step if she wanted to get the object back. It was a little like dealing with her cousin when she was little and he had something she wanted. During his mean phase he would pretend to offer it to her, and then raise it out of reach or throw it somewhere nasty and watch her scuttle after it. Fortunately that phase hadn't lasted very long, but the memory clung. Joellen had a feeling Chris might be going through that kind of phase himself. Was he capable of tossing it out to sea just to spite her?

Keeping her distance so that she didn't get in his face, she made herself into a silent and efficient gatherer of firewood. By the time the fire was blazing and they had to wait for it to die down, she decided she had earned the right to handle the object again. Box. That was how she regarded it, even though it didn't seem to have a lid or any crack indicating that it could be opened. As soon as Chris extended his hand, she yielded it up to him without a fuss.

He tapped it as she had, turned it over, and tapped again. "I'll grant you this," he finally admitted. "It's not wood. Anyway, not wood I've ever seen." Abruptly he rose and walked to the water.

Caught off guard by his suddenness, she had to run to

catch up. She would have begged him if she thought it would do any good. She would have grabbed it if she thought she could get away with it. Anything, oh, anything but let him cast it out to sea.

He stepped onto the long sloping rock, bent down, immersed the object, and scrubbed it on the gravelly bottom.

Joellen watched mud cloud up around it. Was he doing this out of spite or stupidity? She couldn't keep still. "You may be destroying valuable evidence," she told him.

That made him laugh. "You watch too much TV," he said. She was back to being a pain in the butt. To show her how unimpressed he was, he splashed a few yards seaward, the icy water wicking up his pant legs. That didn't stop her, so he waited until she was nearly up to him and then dropped the stupid thing into the drink.

She drew a ragged breath and dived in after it. Groping in the mud she had stirred up, she finally felt one hard edge. It bounced a couple of times before she closed in on it and came up breathless and spluttering with rage.

"Hey," he said, following her back to shore, "it's not my fault. How was I to guess you'd do a damn fool thing like that?"

Clutching the box with both arms and pressing it against her middle, she glared at him. "You just blew it," she said. "You don't deserve to find out what's inside."

"Inside!" he retorted. "You don't even know that there is an inside." He had been alarmed when she stayed underwater so long. Now he was just plain ripped. "You know what you are?" he declared. "You're trouble. Trouble with a big *T*. You going to blame this on me when your father wants to know how you got all wet?"

Shivering, she turned her back on him and stepped as

close to the fire as she dared. As soon as she began to feel the heat blasting her front, she opened her arms to let it in. She didn't trust him enough to turn around and expose the box, which she clutched in one hand, ready to duck away in an instant.

The hell with her, he thought. She was just another spoiled rich kid from away, a little princess who was used to getting anything she wanted. The only way to deal with her was to ignore her.

He stalked off to gather rockweed, then fetched two more armloads before dumping any on the fire. That was to give her a chance to warm up some, but she didn't seem to notice that he was being considerate. The hell with her, he told himself again. When he finally laid the rockweed on the fire, steam rushed up with such force that both he and Joellen were forced to step back.

Joellen shut her eyes, which were tearing from salt and now from smoke as well. At the same time she drew the box closer, holding it in both hands. There was something different. It wasn't as smooth to the touch. Now she could detect with her fingertips a kind of ridge or line running from edge to edge.

Stealthily she turned aside from Chris, who was laying clams on the bed of rockweed. She wiped her nose and eyes on her sleeve, which was warm, though saturated with salt water. Her vision was slow to clear, and she had to stifle the urge to call to Chris to come and look at the amazing thing that was revealing itself to her. She needed to share it with him, or anyway with someone.

She was shivering again. She couldn't stop. Finally, as the box swam into focus, it seemed to change before her eyes. She rubbed them again. That only made them sting even more. What was happening was so magical that she simply forgot to breathe. The stuff that the box was made of had begun to buckle. As if she had dreamed it. No, not dreamed, because you couldn't design a dream. As if she had willed it. A seam emerged the length of the box. There. A seam that might be pried open to reveal—what?

"Chris!" With her breath gone, she had to spit out his name.

But he had had enough of her games. He didn't bother to look up until he had finished covering the clams. "Ah," he sighed, inhaling. So it took him by surprise when she appeared to be thrusting the object under his nose.

Getting no reaction, she grabbed his hand and pressed it on the box.

"What the— Jeez!" he exclaimed. "Look at that."

She nodded, her eyes still tearing but with a big grin plastered across her face. "No," she said. "You look at it. I already did."

19

Chris couldn't get anywhere with his knife. Afraid he would break the big blade, he tried to open the seam with the small one. And all the time he puzzled over the material he was handling, returning again and again to the idea of a shell.

Once a big snapping turtle had preyed on his mother's ducks. He had watched his father catch it and chop off its head. Dad had warned him to keep out of range of the jaws because they were still capable of snapping. Chris had given the severed head a wide berth. But having heard that tortoise-shell was rare and valuable, he had gone after the body. The instant he had grabbed the hard, ridged shell, powerful, scaly limbs had struck at him. It wasn't those dragonlike talons that had freaked him out so much as the headless turtle's sense of him as enemy. He thought of that now as the square object resisted all his efforts to pry it apart.

Joellen had had enough cold water for one day, so she had no intention of hanging around to help Chris pick mussels on the falling tide. But could she trust him with the box? She hung around long enough to get some sense of how he was handling it now that he realized it was something made. When she was pretty sure that he was being careful as well as keen, she promised to bring a screwdriver back from the boat after supper. If Chris brought the box to the lighthouse later, they could work on it this evening.

So they parted on new terms, not quite friends, yet joined in a common goal to uncover whatever secret the mysterious box contained.

Joellen couldn't wait to look at her notebook. Had she already written about the treasure or clue, or had she just thought of it? She needed to go back to the stranger now and decide whether he was friend or foe. She had to know the crime the girl had witnessed. Or was thought to have witnessed. It was time to spell out the danger that stalked any unwary kid, especially in a world without radios, telephones, or inboard engines and outboard motors.

And what about the girl's name? For some reason, Joellen felt she could no longer put off knowing it. But every old-fashioned name that came to mind sounded wrong. Rose was too formal, Lily too limp, Clarissa too fancy. No name seemed to fit.

By the time Joellen sat down with her notebook to cross out one thing and insert another and to pick up the many threads she had left dangling so far, she thought she had made progress. She didn't mind that she would have to rewrite a lot of the beginning. She just couldn't deal with it now, when there wasn't enough space on the first pages for big changes. The main thing, she realized, was to move ahead to the treasure that the bad guy wanted and that the girl unwittingly possessed.

Supper seemed to take forever. Dad and Abbie had an endless discussion about whether they should go somewhere so that Dad could talk to a guy who had already conducted this kind of puffin experiment on another, smaller island. He needed to review some data that would be available on a computer.

"We could use some fresh fruit and bread, too," Abbie remarked.

Joellen said, "If you go to Ledgeport, can you get one of those flashlights that go on your head?"

"If we go to Ledgeport," said Dad, "you're coming with us."

"No!" she blurted. "Why?"

"Because leaving you alone here is out of the question," he told her. "Anyway, I thought you were bored out of your mind here."

"Not anymore," she said. "My story's beginning to work out."

"Good," he replied. "I'm glad to hear it. If we do go, I don't think it'll have to be all the way to the mainland to find a modem. Anyway, I'd like to wrap things up here by the end of the week."

"Are you sure"—she continued craftily, choosing her words with care—"you wouldn't leave me if it was only for a few hours and not overnight?"

Dad shook his head. "What if something happened? I mean, even to us. You'd be stranded here."

She had been lounging on the bunk. Now she sat bolt upright. "That's it!" she shouted. "That's how it happens."

"How what happens?" he asked, smiling at her.

She couldn't tell him that he had just blown her story out of the water. Now she could see what the girl could not know, that she had not been abandoned, not really. Something terrible had happened to the people who intended to return for her. She had no way of learning that. "It's my story," Joellen said. "Could you take me back now? I just figured something out, and I need to write it down."

"Here," said Abbie, handing her a pad. "Will this help?"

It would. It did. Joellen took it into the cockpit. But that wasn't private enough, so she went to sit on the foredeck. She wrote: "At the same time every day the girl went to the tip of the headland and looked out past the ledges toward islands and past them toward where she thought the mainland must be. When would they come for her? How long must she wait? Whenever she sighted a boat in the distance, she waved as hard as she could, but no one paid any attention. Only one person was aware of her presence there. He was in no hurry, though, because he knew that she could not escape him. She was as trapped as an animal in a pit. And the longer she waited, the easier it would be to take her."

Joellen glanced up from the pad. Puffins, looking like bathtub toys, bobbed in the water near the boat. A few black guillemots floated around them, each kind of bird ignoring the other. One took to the air with a fish dangling and was instantly set upon by a great black-backed gull. The puffin, dwarfed by its fierce attacker, dropped the fish and flapped its tiny wings as other gulls joined the pursuit. Jumping to her feet and waving the pad, Joellen yelled, "Hey, pick on someone your own size!"

The gulls ignored her shout, but it brought her father up the companionway to shut her up. "Okay," he said, exasperated with her for breaching his hands-off policy yet again, "I'll row you in. Get what you want from below."

She ripped off the paper she had used, folded it, and handed the pad over to him. "Just my jacket," she said. "I already put stuff in the pockets." At his frown she remembered to add, "Tell Abbie thanks." By then she was back in the cockpit, uncleating the painter and pulling the dinghy alongside *Dovekie*.

20

Chris was waiting outside the lighthouse, his rolled sleeping bag by the open bulkhead.

She was on the verge of asking whether he was planning to move in when his look stopped her. "You got it open!" she exclaimed. "How? What's inside?"

He pulled it from within the sleeping bag, and she saw at once that the box was busted. But it was mostly still intact, she realized on closer inspection. The raised and broken section revealed another layer beneath it.

"I smashed it on the rocks," he told her. "Part of it cracked, and I was able to snap it off." He had not acted out of temper. It had been a measure of last resort, which, when it produced real results, frightened him a little. Even though he was then tempted to repeat this violent approach, he was afraid of breaking more than the outside of the thing.

She examined the edge of the top layer. She had a passing thought that her father might be able to identify the substance. But she knew Chris wouldn't agree to showing it, at least not yet. Anyway, first things first. It was more important to get to the inside of this mysterious box than to learn what it was made of.

They took turns, sometimes with the screwdriver, sometimes with the small knife blade. As they flaked off more pieces from the raised and broken section, they kept probing underneath to feel for the next seam. It took a lot of peeling before it finally came to them that the layer was continuous. The shell-like cover wasn't a lid at all. It was a wrapping.

They were huddled close together, neither one of them willing to let the other dig too far or pull too hard. "Careful," they kept warning, each ready to pounce on the thing, to have another go at it.

"What if it's a trick?" Chris said while Joellen gripped it between her knees so that she could insert the screwdriver under a thicker portion that had the look of folded material. "It could be a practical joke," he went on as the thing slid from her knee grasp and popped free. He held it for her, trying to keep it from bending under pressure.

"You mean, nothing inside?" she responded. "Who would go to all this trouble? Especially since whoever put it where we found it couldn't have known about us."

Chris shook his head. "A joke on someone else," he said. "Someone that was supposed to find it and feel—" He broke off. Joellen had managed to pry back the thicker fold and with it yet another layer that came free at the same time. "Light!" he ordered. "Let's see it in the light."

She held it up. Here the clear sky, still bright, showed

them what they had craved to find. Chris snatched it from Joellen and called for her flashlight.

"Get it yourself," she told him. "You know where it is."

But he wasn't about to walk away from it any more than she was.

So they worked on enlarging the opening, the suspense almost unbearable now that they knew for sure that something was really in there. The last inner layer, which seemed to belong to the outer shell, was less brittle and easier to handle. They didn't even need to tear it apart. It simply yielded to their hands to expose a small book. Chris held the wrapping out while Joellen reached inside and took the book between her fingers. Except for some yellowish streaks, all color had leached from the binding, which was deceptively soft to the touch until she opened the book. Then she felt the stiffness of its pages.

It was a journal. It began with a date: "11 September, 1848." And then it read, "I Patrick Healy, schoolmaster, with some misgivings yet with hope, commence this day a journey with my wife, Lucy, and her sister, Flora, a child of ten years, and their mother, all lately of Ardtully in County Kerry, Ireland, to seek a new life in America. . . ."

"But what about this?" Joellen demanded, pointing to a note in the margin above the date. "It says, 'Urgent! Go to back of book.'"

"We will, we will," Chris told her. "This thing's waited, what, nearly one hundred and fifty years. A few minutes more won't matter. Let's see what this Patrick Healy's got to say for himself."

He turned one page and began to read out loud. "'I have closed my school with regret, knowing that my few remaining scholars rely on the food I have provided with their studies. It is a bitter thing to keep back savings for the sake of family when hunger and misery are everywhere. Knowing of the vile conditions aboard the coffin ships, I attempted to purchase two cabins. Alas, I could secure but one small space abovedecks. It is intended for two passengers, but we four will share the cramped quarters and will count ourselves among the fortunate. These ships take on far more human cargo than they can carry. It is widely reported that many passengers, already weak from starvation, fail to survive the voyage.'"

"What starvation? What's he talking about?" Chris asked.

"Maybe slaves," Joellen said. "It's how they crammed people into slave ships."

Chris scowled. He turned back the page and read the date again, 1848. "But he isn't a slave. He bought space abovedecks. He has money."

"So we can read the rest after we go to the back," Joellen told him. "Come on, Chris, this is mine, too. It's urgent."

He didn't argue. He handed the book to her, and she turned it over. Here was the urgent thing, a message from Patrick Healy to—She expected it to begin, "Dear so-and-so," but it didn't. Nor did it resemble the neat script of the journal entries she and Chris had read. "It's someone else!" she declared. "See? The handwriting's different." She struggled to decipher the scrawl.

" 'We are in thrall to a Mr. Hardison, whom I first looked upon with favor when he came in the dark to our ship as we waited at anchor in St. John Harbor. Now I perceive that Mr. Hardison is a man driven by greed who preys upon desperate people. His mate, a Mr. Smythe or Smite, tells me they regularly offer to passengers who can meet the

115

price an entry into the United States, passengers otherwise condemned to Canadian quarantine in fever sheds, where many die.'

"St. John?" Joellen said, interrupting her reading. "Where's that?"

"It's in Canada, not very far down the coast from here. See what else he says."

Joellen read on. " 'Mr. Hardison has arranged with certain seamen on ships from Ireland to bring him passengers who can pay well to escape quarantine and be set ashore in the United States. During the first weeks of our journey my wife's younger sister and her mother had shared our small space abovedecks. Upon discovery they were sent below, where, after many more weeks in that foul hold crowded with fever victims, my wife's mother succumbed.' "

Joellen tilted the page to catch the fading light. "So he is the same person."

"Right. With a wife and her little sister like at the start. Only now the mother-in-law's dead," Chris added, taking over the reading.

" 'Accepting Mr. Hardison's terms, I insisted on only half payment at the outset and the remainder upon our safe delivery. I now suspect that Mr. Hardison's ready agreement may have concealed—' " Chris struggled with the scrawls at the bottom of the page.

"Just keep reading," Joellen said. "We can come back to the hard parts."

" ' . . . fearing to endure one more trial,' " he continued haltingly, grasping at any phrase he could decipher, " 'suspecting no villainy. . . . With little time to reflect. . . . Such privation had left her in a sorry state and . . . I had no choice.' "

The next page was an improvement. Even in the waning light Chris was able to read about the others, a man and his two sons, who fell prey to Mr. Hardison's scheme to arrange immediate entry into the United States. " 'So after nearly three long months at sea, we six were secreted aboard a small boat with scant protection from the weather. Only Mr. Hardison and Mr. Smythe wore oilskins. Lucy and Flora huddled beneath a canvas cover, but were soon as drenched as the rest of us.' "

"Boat people!" Joellen exclaimed, figuring three months from early September. "And it must have been November by then." She shivered at the thought. "Let's go inside," she said. "We need the flashlight now anyway."

"How about staying out and making a fire instead?"

A fire sounded wonderful. But then she thought of her father. A fire on this headland would bring him here in an instant. "Are you ready to meet my dad?" she asked Chris.

"No!" Chris said.

Joellen nodded. "Besides, he'd make us put it out."

"Why?" Chris demanded. "What gives him the right—"

"Nothing can interfere with the puffin environment. Especially fire."

Chris shook his head. "You buy that? It's like puffins are more important than people."

Joellen laughed. "You can say that again." But a moment later, groping through the dark for the stairs, she mulled over his question and said, "I don't know. I don't know where I stand about a lot of stuff like that." Come to think of it, she couldn't even be sure where her father stood now that he had moved on, leaving his old family behind in his past. It was as though the entire world had tilted, setting everything she thought she understood at a precarious angle.

117

She felt in her pocket for a candy bar and was about to help herself to it when she remembered that Chris would refuse her offer to share. Pigheaded, she thought, withdrawing her hand as stealthily as she could to keep from rattling the candy wrapper and giving herself away.

21

When they were settled, she took over the reading. "'We sailed through the night and into the day, beating against a punishing wind. As the weather worsened, I pleaded with Mr. Hardison to seek some harbor where we might wait out the storm. But he said that any landfall this close to the border would put us all at risk. At length he sought shelter on an offshore island where rough seas prevented our landing near a lighthouse and dwelling. We skirted the island until we gained entry into a protected cove.'

"Where?" Joellen said. "Which cove?"

"You shouldn't be taken in by something like this," Chris told her. "It could be, you know, like made up."

She shook her head. "It isn't. Look how thick the paper is, and the old-fashioned writing. Listen to what else he says here." She went on. " 'But Mr. Hardison failed to reckon on the crosscurrents and and violent seas, and his boat fetched up on an offshore ledge, swept broadside before we could safely land. All was in shambles, Mr. Hardison rescuing gear while I assisted my wife. Her sister held fast to the boat as it broke up. By the time I was able to return for her, she had been hurled upon the rocks, injuring her face and leg.'

"Not here then," Joellen said. "It sounds more like Dread Mans Cove."

Chris shook his head. "They'd never have climbed up and out." He paused, thinking about the constant assault of waves and tides on the cliff face. "Unless the cove was a lot different back then. I don't know if it could change that much in a hundred and fifty years."

Joellen resumed the reading. " 'I wished to bring her across the island to shelter, but Mr. Hardison declared that if the keeper proved a law-abiding man, he must turn us over to the authorities. And if he were not, it would go even harder for us, since the lightkeepers on these islands earn so mean a livelihood that some actually hold storm victims hostage for gain. As we still have some of our clothing and my waterproof bag with my purse, this journal, and a few of my wife's mementos, and as Mr. Hardison has determined to approach the lightkeeper without divulging our national-ity, we have left him to it. Only now I wonder how else it might benefit him to keep our identity secret while arrang-ing to have us transported to the mainland.

" 'Mr. Smythe and I had strength to bring wood for a fire, but the other gentleman and his sons could do nothing, being numb with cold and exhaustion.

" 'Mr. Smythe seems pitifully grateful for my kind use of him. As companions in misery we have come to an understanding. Perhaps he hopes to avert an even greater calamity than we have thus far experienced. This much he has revealed: that Mr. Hardison has no means of securing legal entry into the United States for Irish immigrants and that he simply abandons his passengers after final payment.

" 'I write this because Mr. Smythe hints that this time Mr. Hardison may be plotting something more villainous. Now that Mr. Hardison has lost his boat, he must not only distance himself from us to save his lucrative trade, but he must find some means of procuring a replacement vessel.

" 'Mr. Smythe has agreed to request the use of a spade for sanitary purposes, and I shall employ it to dig a hole in which to bury this document. He can also provide a square of oilskin salvaged from the wreck. It is my intention to wrap in it the last of our tokens and keepsakes from home, along with my journal and this report, before concealing the packet in the ground, these to be recovered upon my return for my wife and her sister. In the event that I come to harm, my wife will bring this report to the attention of the authorities. As I do not want her to dwell overlong on my suspicions, I shall wait until we are ready to depart from here before instructing her in this matter.

" 'My hope is that Mr. Hardison and others who smuggle helpless famine victims will be brought to justice, and that we who attempted to circumvent the law will not be judged too severely. All we desired was to save our loved ones and ourselves from further hardship and likely death.' "

This ended with Patrick Healy's signature and a partial date, "November . . . 1848."

"But there's something more," Chris said. "It shows through the page."

Joellen just sat, though, trying to absorb all that she had

read. It was real. She had no doubt of that. It was a story that was true.

"Go on," Chris told her. Then he took the book and the flashlight out of her hands, turned the page, and started to read. " 'A change of plans. Lucy may not stay. As I left the lighthouse to return to our makeshift encampment here, she was still pleading not to be parted from Flora, who has grown worse and has taken no nourishment, even though Mr. Hardison brought from the keeper's farm better food than we have eaten in months.

" 'Mr. Hardison remains firm in his resolve. He was indignant at my wife's insistence that she remain. Wasn't it hard enough that he had lost his boat trying to rescue a few Irish? Her presence in the keeper's household, even for a day or two, would lead to questions. His arrangement would be compromised, and we would be sent straightaway to quarantine and denied entry into this country.

" 'But Lucy is distraught. Flora's mangled foot requires medical attention. The keeper mentioned an excellent hospital, but it is some distance. The child is too fevered to withstand further travel, especially as the wind has given over to bitter cold. The keeper's wife will tend her. Despite Mr. Hardison's order of silence, while I carried the child into the house I quickly informed the keeper's wife about the hole I have prepared beneath the great oak that stands in the meadow. I have assured her that she will find it but loosely filled and easily reopened. That is all I can do to ease her of the burden I have thrust upon her, since I must needs depend upon her in the event my worst fears come to pass. She has promised that all will be seen to.

" 'If it is you, kind lady, who first reads these words, we are in your debt. Yet at the last, I take heart. For even as I

122

mistrust Mr. Hardison for insisting that Lucy join us in the keeper's boat so that all of us who are sensible of him are together, it seems unlikely we will come to harm as long as we are in the company of the lightkeeper.

" 'And now I must fold this indictment and journal, along with a few keepsakes from our former lives, into the square of oilskin Mr. Smythe has provided. As I hasten to join the others, who await me, perhaps already in the lightkeeper's boat, I shall display the pouch I left behind when I carried Flora across the island to the house. It was my pretext for returning here and has given me the opportunity to add these few lines before burying the oilskin packet and filling in the hole.' " This time there was no signature. Chris's voice just fell away.

After a time night sounds intruded, the occasional challenge of a gull or the eruption of a quarrel somewhere among the birds. Joellen removed the paper she had written on, then didn't look at it. She wondered why Chris hadn't turned off the flashlight, but she didn't say anything about it.

Finally he spoke. "So everything must have worked out for them."

"That's what you want to think," she told him.

"Maybe they came back for the girl and there wasn't time to get his stuff."

Joellen didn't reply.

"Why not?" he argued. "If anything bad happened, the lightkeeper's wife would've dug this all up and so it wouldn't be there for us to find."

Joellen unfolded the sheet of paper and placed it on his knees. He tilted the flashlight and began to read.

"Not out loud," she said, clapping her hands over her ears.

"What is this?" he demanded. "Where's this from?"

"It's part of my story."

"This is a joke. Right?"

Joellen shook her head. "I wrote it after supper. Just about everything I write seems to, you know, like come true."

"Jeez!" he murmured. He read on silently to the end. Then he said, "Are you trying to tell me that you know what happened to her? To them? You can't expect me to buy that."

Joellen shook her head again. "No, I don't know. I wish I did. I don't know where my story's going either."

"Well," he declared, setting the book and flashlight aside and rising, "if that's what it's like to have an imagination, I'm glad I don't."

"You do," she said. "Everyone does."

"Not that kind. Not like you and my grandfather. The two of you sound like refugees from the Twilight Zone."

"Oh!" she exclaimed, not even registering the intended insult. "Do you think your grandfather's stories have anything to do with . . . this?"

"Listen," Chris told her from somewhere near the doorway to the stairs, "I don't think anything, except that you could've come across Spars Island gossip and stories somewhere." He paused. "If your dad spoke to mine about sheep and stuff, maybe you even met my grandad."

"I don't think so," she said. "Anyway, what could he have told me?"

Chris was embarrassed, but he couldn't get out of telling her. "Weird stuff. That this place is like haunted. There's supposed to be a ghost that has it in for . . . some people."

"Go on," she said.

"I can't," he answered, retreating as he spoke. "That's all there is to it. It's like a superstition to do with an ancestor of mine, ancient history."

"Where are you going?" she asked him.

"To the cellar hole. I brought my sleeping bag this time. I'll pick up the book in the morning and be out of here before your dad comes ashore."

She started to protest. He didn't have sole claim to the book. Far from it. But she had a lot to ponder. And she might do some more reading on her own. After all, she had a good supply of flashlight batteries in reserve.

22

Groaning with relief, Chris crawled into the sleeping bag. It felt good to know that he would be warm enough to sleep through the night. He was glad this day was over. Tomorrow he would concentrate on what really mattered: food. He was ready for a change of diet. After clamming he ought to hunt for strawberries out on Folly Point. There might be a few ripe fruits in the crevices where years of sheep grazing enriched the thin soil.

Folly Point was the only true grassland on Fowlers Island, the nearest thing to meadow. Yet Patrick Healy had mentioned walking through a meadow to reach the lighthouse dwelling. Come to think of it, he had implied that the oak stood prominently in open land. Did that mean that he was a phony? Could he have made everything up? After all, that was what Joellen was doing in her story. And it was practically one and the same thing.

Chris rolled over and rested his face on his folded arms. Forget it, he told himself. Get it out of your mind.

But he couldn't stop trying to find reasonable explanations for facts that didn't mesh. Like the meadow. Maybe it wasn't that hard to figure out. In his aunt's shop there were plenty of old pictures of Spars and Coombes and other islands, maybe even this one, though he couldn't be sure of that.

People from away paid good money for faded photos from the past that showed familiar places you'd hardly recognize. Before the fish plants had shut down on Spars, there had been a real village around its crowded harbor, with drying yards and an icehouse and stores and two churches. For a while Mom had let him keep a picture on his wall showing a square-rigged bark unloading salt for the fish factory. And when the quarry on Coombes was shipping tons of granite down the coast, the island was even busier than Spars. Pictures of schooners loaded with paving stone and of the cutting yards and polishing mill were big items in the shop where she worked.

All the islands had changed. A century and more ago those that were farmed had open pasture and haylands. Now they were grown to forest, mostly spruce, but with some hardwoods as well.

So what did this prove about Patrick Healy?

Chris turned on his side, the sleeping bag twisting under him and binding his legs. What was he doing here anyway? Why wasn't he at home with the TV and something real to eat and the telephone? Was he beginning to go off the deep end?

It was hard to tell whether it helped to have someone else witness the journal and accusation. Joellen wasn't exactly reliable. Still, she was pretty sharp.

What did she mean with that question about Grandad's stuff if she hadn't ever heard about the ghost girl? Chris couldn't believe that he had held out on her about the ghost being a girl. After all, he had nothing to hide.

Or was Joellen on to something?

The only thing Chris could be sure of was that he had long since outgrown ghosts. That flickering light the first night? Come to find out Joellen was up near the lighthouse with her flashlight. If it had made him think he heard some sort of voice, too, that was only natural. After all, Grandad had filled him full of that haunting stuff when he was little and ignorant. As for the head in the mirror with all the hair, well, there had to be some reason for it. Anyway, he hadn't freaked out. He had just decided to avoid confusion. Who wouldn't, in all that fog?

Chris squirmed free of the sleeping bag, sat up, and pulled it over his shoulders. What bugged him now was that he couldn't recollect exactly which part about the Fowlers Island haunting was actual history and which part was superstition. Some of it was connected to what happened to Grandad. But of course he couldn't have a memory of it himself, since he was only three years old when his mother and brother drowned off Fowlers Island.

Mom called it hearsay. Mom said that Grandad's grandmother filling his head full of nonsense was like brainwashing. She said he ought to know better than to pass it on to his own innocent grandson.

Innocent! Chris grinned to himself. Had Mom really said that, or was he rehashing it that way? Mom hated it when

128

Chris came home from spending time with Grandad and recounted events that never happened.

"Did so happen," Dad declared one time, though he usually stayed out of it.

"How can you say that?" Mom had objected. "You can't just sit there and encourage your kid to go along with an old man's brainless ghost stories."

Dad had turned to her then. "It's not all brainless. There's plenty over to Spars that know about it. People that know him and knew her, too. She was a powerful person there. Besides," he had added, "the way I heard it, Dad's grandmother never did make any claims about a ghost. All that came along afterward."

"You mean she didn't start all those rumors?"

"I mean," Dad said, "even if it started with her, it took off from what really happened and how she saw things. It was even written up in that book about the islands. You know, the one you and Nancy sell in her shop."

That had stopped Mom, but not for long. "Still, a lot of it's hearsay. No one has proof."

"There were eyewitness accounts of the boat capsizing," Dad had reminded her. "Everyone in the other boat saw it happen."

This was more or less where Chris had stopped listening. He had heard it before. He was to hear it again, whenever Mom rebuked Grandad for turning a family tragedy into a ghost story that could only lead to nightmares.

But as the familiar events played back inside Chris's head, fragments of scenes and scraps of phrases rose to the surface of his thoughts. Like storm-flung kelp or sea wrack floating half submerged, weighted by the stones on which they were rooted, the words bobbed and slipped from his grasp.

He told himself not to try so hard. Think of bringing back a song you could almost but not quite sing. It might come into your head after you had given up and were into something else.

He got up and shook out the sleeping bag. Something clattered away, possibly what was left of the oilskin wrapping he had stuffed inside the bag. Only whatever it was bounced off the rocky ground like metal.

He paused. If it wasn't the shell-like oilskin, then how had it got in his sleeping bag? And if it was in his sleeping bag, why hadn't it fallen out when he unrolled it here in the first place?

He dropped onto his knees and began to sweep the area with both hands. He found whatever it was almost at once where it had come to rest against the wall. He didn't have to see it to confirm that it was metal. Hard metal, so maybe not a coil from a bedspring, which is what he first assumed. His next guess was that it came from the old stock fence that his father used to shore up this pen when he had to hold sheep. That rusted fencing was so heavy it was a misery to bend and use, but it was strong enough to keep the wild island sheep from busting free. Chris nodded to himself as he fingered the wire and tossed it back against the wall. He didn't want it to snag and rip his sleeping bag.

He was winding down now, just about ready to let the questions go. After crawling back inside the sleeping bag, he stretched full length and wiggled his feet to make sure he had enough room to move. It felt good to have solved the small puzzle of the metal ring with a simple, down-to-earth solution. All you had to do really was deal with facts as you saw them.

On the brink of sleep, Grandad spoke out of his own past. Something about the fierce child left on the island. Fierce. That was the word Grandad said his grandmother had used, not once but many times. The child, left behind, sad and fierce she is, that child waiting there. Fierce.

23

In the profound darkness before dawn even the usually raucous gulls were silent on their roosts. But Joellen was instantly awake and tense with expectation. She listened. All that came to her ears was the rhythmic whisper of the sea as it surged against the rocky shore.

She reached for her flashlight and Patrick Healy's journal. Turning to the beginning, she began to read the part they had skipped. It was different from the wordy introduction and even more different from the report at the end, which was written in pencil. These entries were in ink and written with what he called a steel pen. Most of them were brief accounts entered every few days and written in the cramped shelter the shipping agent had sold him as a cabin. Sometimes no more than a phrase or two were jotted down.

The tone grew bitter after Flora and her mother had been evicted and sent below. He offered to pay an additional fee for them, but the captain would not allow more than two persons in each shelter. "He thinks nothing of packing human cargo in the hold. So jammed are they below, only some may stretch out at a time."

Gradually a picture emerged, not only of Patrick Healy and his bride, Lucy, but of the country from which they had fled. With another failure of the potato crop, on which almost everyone depended, famine and disease overwhelmed the already weakened population. People died in ditches beside the roads leading to ports from which emigration ships embarked. Lucy had tried to save a baby found in the arms of its dead mother, but she had no way to feed the starving infant, which lived only a few hours longer.

Once aboard ship, Lucy concentrated on her mother's failing health. During the first two weeks, most of Patrick Healy's entries dealt with food and the dwindling supplies of medicine they carried. But they also contained a few revealing remarks about Lucy's younger sister, Flora, with words like *irrepressible* and *boisterous* to describe her. Reading between the lines, Joellen guessed that Flora was driving her brother-in-law up the wall.

Yet when she and her mother were forced to go below, he did everything in his power to rescue them, including offering to take his mother-in-law's place. He documented every breach of what he called the Passenger Acts, laws that required ships to provide seven pounds of food for each passenger every week. Even the water supplied to passengers abovedecks eventually became undrinkable.

But his rage reached new heights when he learned two days after his wife's mother had died that her remains had been dumped into the ocean along with several others who had died around the same time. For a while he feared that Flora was also gone. Lucy was frantic, Flora being the last surviving member of her once-large family.

At last, toward the end of the journal, Joellen came to a full description of Flora after she was found. "She is not herself. She barely speaks. She seems shrunken, if that be possible. She was always just a slip of a girl, but abundant in spirit. Now her eyes appear bruised and dull, and she is altogether careless of her person. As I write, Lucy bathes her face and works to disentangle her snarled and befouled hair, which once shone black as sea coal.

"The ship's hand who fetched Flora from that hellish hold cannot betray us without risk to himself. But it has cost us dear, and he did attempt to keep her bracelet, which slipped from her arm when he carried her to us. Lucy would not hear of this, the object being a gift from her father, who found it while cutting turf in the bog. We convinced the fellow that had it any value beyond sentiment, it would have been stolen long since. But I believe it to be bronze and of ancient origin. I will hold it in safe keeping with her horn spoon until we are settled ashore."

Joellen paused here, then flipped past the last journal page and several blank ones to the penciled scrawl at the back. She had to turn the book over to read the message written on this island in 1848. Here again were the passages she hadn't been able to read. Skimming over them, she hunted for Patrick Healy's reference to other things to be wrapped and buried with his journal. Here it was. Tokens. That's what he called them. Tokens and keepsakes.

So where were they then? What had become of them? Was it possible that someone had dug up the wrapped book, taken the things, and then reburied it? But who would do that? Mr. Hardison? Maybe that man Smythe had told on Patrick Healy, and Mr. Hardison had come back for whatever of value could be had. But why would Mr. Hardison bury the journal again? Why not just burn it or drop it in the sea?

Joellen racked her brains. There had to be another answer. This wasn't panning out right.

She set the journal aside and looked all around as though this one room contained a hidden answer. She noticed that while she was reading, morning had dawned. She switched off the flashlight.

If this were a story, she thought, there might be a hint right under her nose. Stories like treasure hunts provided clues when you needed them, whereas real life was just a great swamp with every possible escape route leading to one dead end after another.

Her eye fell to her notebook. Maybe that was the next thing to do. She could pick it up and start writing and just see how the thread of her story unraveled.

But she didn't want to touch it, not now anyway. In some mysterious way Patrick's account and her own story had grown uncomfortably close.

She didn't understand how it had happened. She only knew that making things up had become a dangerous game. She couldn't trust what she wrote; it was too much like a mirror bolted to rocks to trick and bemuse ungrounded puffins. Until Patrick Healy's story was complete, until she found out exactly what had happened to him and Lucy and Flora, she didn't dare tinker with her own characters. It was one thing when they had been nameless and formless. Now she knew that when she wrote again, the girl would have a name: Flora. It was all she could add for now. But if Flora, then there must be Lucy and Patrick and Smythe and Mr. Hardison, for they were all connected.

If only they were just characters, she thought. She might make Lucy scratch a message into the glass window or maybe even leave it on the thick lens in the lighthouse tower. That could be intriguing. Mr. Hardison would never think of looking in such an out-of-the-way place for evidence that could expose him.

But if they were merely characters that existed in her mind and on the pages of her notebook, it would be too easy to lose control of the game and its consequences. The way her father did when he had to stand by while black-backed gulls circled above the burrows from which puffin chicks would soon emerge to their peril, chicks five years in the making and finally planted upon this island.

24

"I'm off," Chris called to Joellen from the stairs. "I think your father's getting ready to row ashore."

"Oh," Joellen answered. "Did he see you?"

"Of course not. I just noticed that he'd pulled up the dinghy. You want to toss me the book?"

"No, Chris, of course not. You don't throw something this old."

"Bull," he said, appearing in the doorway. "Where is it?"

But when she handed it to him and he grabbed it by the spine, the covers flew wide. Out from between blank pages dropped two small objects. Chris caught one of them in the air. The other fluttered to Joellen's feet, landing awkwardly like a maimed bird.

She stopped, then carefully lifted what looked like a

paper wing. It was nothing but a scrap of folded paper containing a lock of hair. The hair was brown and dry. There was something creepy about its being from someone long dead. Quickly she tucked it inside its packet, which bore no name, no date. Clearly Patrick Healy, who must have placed it there, believed that neither Lucy nor Flora needed it identified.

"What's that other thing?" she asked Chris.

He couldn't say. He just held up a picture mounted on a round of lace. At first she thought it was an old-fashioned valentine. But there were no hearts or flowers or verse, only a side view of a head in solid black, a kind of portrait of a young woman or girl wearing a bonnet.

"Lucy!" Joellen exclaimed.

"How do you know it's not Flora?" Chris responded.

She was about to tell him that Flora was just a slip of a girl when he darted a nervous glance over his shoulder. He wanted to get away before Dad and Abbie arrived. Instead she said, "Maybe you should leave these things here. In case of rain or something."

To her surprise he gave her no argument, only insisting that he know where she planned to hide them.

"In my notebook," she said. "I can leave it under one of those old barrels."

"But you'll want it for your story," he objected.

She shook her head. "Not now. I'm not writing any more for a while."

She opened the notebook to clean pages at the back and placed the hair and the portrait inside. Then she followed him down to the lighthouse cellar and waited for him to climb out so that light through the bulkhead would show her the way to the barrels in the dark recess of the foundation wall.

It was beginning to register with her that Flora's bracelet and a spoon were missing. She ran to the bulkhead stairs and shouted up to Chris, who was just shouldering his sleeping bag.

"Where's the oilskin?"

"I'm pretty sure I cleaned up all the pieces," he called back.

"But the big part," she said. "What we pulled the book out of."

"It's here," he answered. "In my sleeping bag."

"Can I see it?"

"Not now, Joellen. They're coming."

"Just leave it," she pleaded, certain that the missing objects must be jammed down inside the boxlike wrap.

He muttered something, sounding mildly annoyed. Then he said, "It's here. Don't leave it for them to see."

"No," she told him, "I'll put it with the journal. Thanks, Chris."

She retrieved it from the top step and then sat outside to get the full benefit of the light. She peered inside. Nothing. Maybe the keepsakes were concealed between the last two layers of oilskin that Chris had bent back until they broke. She pressed every way she could, but found no suggestive lump.

She was at a loss to come up with any answer that made sense. Someone had taken the bracelet and spoon. If it was Patrick Healy, he might have reburied the notebook quickly when he realized he had been followed to the oak tree. Only why would he have been so anxious to conceal what he had written? Because he had been wrong about Mr. Hardison?

Right or wrong, if Patrick Healy had made it safely back to Fowlers Island for Flora, he wouldn't have wanted their illegal entry exposed. Say it was the lightkeeper who came

139

after him, maybe to see if he needed help. Patrick Healy would have been quick to hide the evidence.

Joellen could hear Dad and Abbie talking as they approached. She scuttled down into the dark cellar, shoved her notebook and the broken oilskin container under the farthest barrel, and dashed back up to the round room.

"Josie?" Dad called. "Sorry, I mean Joellen. We're leaving. You can have breakfast under way."

"No, John," Abbie said, "I brought her an orange and a couple of biscuits and jam."

They spoke together quietly, just out of earshot. Then Abbie appeared with the food. "Kind of old, these biscuits," she said. "We can stock up at the Coombes store."

"Why aren't we going to Ledgeport?" Joellen asked, disappointed. She was thinking that the library, if it was open today, might have information that would shed some light on what had happened in November 1848.

"Your dad wants to finish up here as soon as possible. We can get to Coombes and back in half the time it would take to go to Ledgeport. He's already radioed around to find a computer he can use. We can be back tonight or first thing tomorrow."

"Weather permitting," Dad added as he joined them. "Better bring your sleeping bag, just in case," Dad told Joellen.

She started to roll it up. "I'd be perfectly fine here," she said. She couldn't help trying, even though he had made himself absolutely clear on the subject of her being left alone on the island even for one night. If only she could tell him that she wasn't exactly alone. But that might make it worse, not better.

"No doubt," he said. "I wouldn't, though."

She considered saying something about needing to know what it was like to be left behind for real. She thought better of it.

"Is that everything?" he asked as she hoisted her knapsack.

"You have your notebook?" Abbie added.

Joellen sort of nodded. They would be back. Meanwhile it was safe enough. The only thing that bothered her was that Chris might get nosy and read it. But he had the real journal to read. Why would he bother with hers? Anyway, he might not even show up at the lighthouse. Still, she ought to leave a note, just in case.

When they left, her dad started to close the bulkhead doors. She convinced him to leave them open to allow fresh air inside for her. She waited until they were well away from the lighthouse before exclaiming that she had forgotten something. She thrust her sleeping bag at Dad, promising to be only a minute. Then she dashed back to scribble a message for Chris on the folded page Abbie had given her from the lined pad. "Back tonight or tomorrow. Don't throw this away. J." She stuck a corner of it inside her notebook where he was bound to see it if he did come looking for her or the "tokens" and "keepsakes." She couldn't wait to hear what he thought of everything once he'd read the rest of the journal.

As she backed out from under the barrel, Joellen's glance picked up the faded black *W* painted on the end. *W* for "winter," if Abbie was right. But she must be. She had come across this bit of information by accident. What was it she had called it? An exhibition.

By the time Joellen reached the ladder she was out of breath from running hard. Dad and Abbie were already in the dinghy. So was her sleeping bag. Panting, she climbed down to the small thwart in the bow. As soon as she was settled with her knapsack at her feet, she looked past her father's back to Abbie, who sat in the stern facing her across the length of the dinghy.

"So," Joellen began, pausing to regain her breath, "would anyone be able to get into that exhibition that has stuff about winter oil and summer oil?"

Abbie became instantly talkative. Whether it was the subject she warmed to or the possibility of making friends with her lover's daughter, Joellen couldn't tell and didn't much care. What came through loud and clear for Joellen was that Abbie could put her in touch with information that might fill in some of the blanks that bound this island story in mystery.

25

Long before the rain started, Chris could feel it coming. The wind was light enough, but it had veered around from south-southeast nearly to east. And the sea had that flat gray surface that made you think of hard, dull sheet metal.

Taking note of this change, Chris rolled the journal inside his foul-weather jacket before going out to gather mussels. He would pick a whole lot to have on hand just in case the wind veered some more. It wasn't likely to turn into a bad nor'easter this time of year, but you could never tell. Well, you couldn't tell unless you had a weather radio or a friend whose father's yacht probably picked up every weather signal along the coast.

Wading out into the swift current where the mussels were big and clean, he had to stand for a moment and suck in his breath to keep from yelping. The water out here must be ten degrees colder than a few yards closer to shore. He thought of the people who had fetched up on these rocks in November. The girl, Flora, had clung to the wreckage of the boat. Not many people could survive immersion for long at this time of year, let alone in late fall or early winter. Think what it must have done to her. Patrick Healy mentioned an injured foot. But what about hypothermia? What would have been done for her in those days?

Chris tugged at rockweed laden with mussels. Soon his arms were full, and he had to carry the load in. It occurred to him as he dropped it above the tide line that mussels would keep longer attached to all this rockweed. How many days had it taken him to figure this out?

The second time in was less of a shock. He didn't even gasp as the water clamped his legs in its icy grip, although it was worse when he had to reach down deep to pull the rockweed. And now there was a passing boat to contend with. He could hear the motor even before he saw it; that meant it would be close enough to send its wake to splash him.

He looked up. It didn't sound like a lobsterman. What kind of nut would fool around with these ledges at low tide?

Then he saw who. Andy and Eric came swinging around the point, churning up water and rockweed as they brought the boat inside the lobster buoys and halted upcurrent with the engine idling.

"So how's it going?" Andy shouted.

"It sucks," Chris called out to them. "A week's too long."

"We should've let Gary go first," Eric said. "Then he could've quit early, and all you'd have to do was stay a little longer than him. As it is, your grandad says we've got to bring you home sooner. Friday, he says."

Chris felt like telling them he didn't care anymore. He wanted to go home now.

"You'll make it," Andy told him. "You don't look like you're starving to death."

"I'm some hungry," Chris responded.

"Lonely?" Eric yelled. "Did you say lonely?"

"No," Chris shouted out to them. "Hungry. Bring a pizza when you come for me."

Andy shut off the engine. The boat bobbed and swung around in the current. "Any messages for your grandfather? He's some fussed about you being out here."

"Tell him I'm fine. Don't tell him I'm hungry."

"Or lonely," Eric added with a grin.

"Well, I can't be lonely. There's people on the other side of the island."

"Cripes!" said Andy. "You getting stuff from them?"

"Of course not. Would I be hungry if I was? Anyway, only one girl knows I'm here."

"A girl!" Both boys hooted.

"Nice going," declared Andy.

"One girl should be enough," said Eric.

"It's not like that," Chris said. "She's just a kid."

"Uh-huh!" said Eric.

"Right," said Andy. "What's she look like?"

"I don't know." Didn't they realize he was standing in a cake of ice? He couldn't feel his legs and feet, and his fingers were going numb, too. "I gotta go," he said.

"Where is she?" Andy demanded.

"I told you. Over to the lighthouse. Off a sloop. What's up with the weather?"

"Rain," said Eric. "Clearing tomorrow. But we might be in for more fog, so you be ready to go at low water Friday. Dead low should be close to one, one-thirty."

"Right." Chris was ready to go this very minute. Stumbling over rocks slippery with weed, he staggered onto the beach and dumped his mussels. Eric had to yank the starter rope a few times before the engine roared. He put it in gear and backed off from one ledge into another. He swore. Both boys were laughing as they headed out and disappeared around the point.

By now Chris was so chilled all he could think of was a fire. There might still be time to dig clams, but first off he needed to get warm. He was shivering so hard he had trouble laying the wood. His fingers were too stiff to handle small bits of kindling. He hoped Joellen didn't show up just now to hear his teeth chattering like hail on a tin roof.

It was a wasteful fire. That meant he would have to pay for it with long hikes inland for more dry wood. At the moment he didn't care. All that mattered was that feeling was painfully returning to his fingers and toes, and the flames were heating up his shirt to the scorching point. It felt wonderful.

He wouldn't have bothered to stop and eat now if it weren't for the coming rain. It might be awhile before he got another such fire going. He would stoke up on hot mussels and steam a bunch more to eat later on.

His idea of hunting for a few ripe strawberries on Folly Point seemed like a screwball notion now that he was getting warm inside his wet clothes. It wouldn't take much of a damp wind out there to start up the chill inside him. So he stayed close to the fire, eating mussels and slurping their salty juices from the shells.

Just going as far as the next beach for clams seemed dumb, but he did it anyway and found on his return that the fire had burned down to embers. He coaxed it into life once more. Then, after bedding it with rockweed and laying on a batch of clams, he watched the rain snake across the island on ribbons of black cloud.

26

Joellen chafed at one delay after another. Even when Dad left the computer for a few minutes, he wouldn't let her near it. Someone was checking into earlier records for him. He had to wait for a reply.

"Can't I just get started?"

Instead of answering her, he turned to his host, an old acquaintance who had kindly made her computer available to him. "Kids today," he declared, "they're dependent on instant communication. Especially," he added, "after a few days on an island."

Joellen set her face in sullen disregard. She would not rise to this bait.

"You're the image of your mother," the host had remarked when they arrived at her door. She had plunged on. "How is Ellen? Where is she?"

Dad had to explain. Joellen had been too embarrassed to note the host's expression. Or Dad's. But of course he breezed through the awkward moment. He always did.

The host had quickly departed from the subject of Joellen's resemblance to her mother. Now she addressed Joellen's impatience. "It's normal at her age," the host said, and then to Joellen, "I'm sure you want to be in touch with your friends."

"Actually," Abbie told her when Joellen failed to respond, "this isn't social. Joellen is looking into the history of Fowlers Island light."

"Oh," said the host, "how interesting."

"Here we go," said Dad as a message appeared on the screen. And for the next few minutes he was completely immersed in his own instant communication.

Joellen caught a look from Abbie, who gestured toward Dad, shook her head, and then rolled her eyes. Almost as if they were in this together.

When Dad finally finished and turned the computer over to Joellen, Abbie stayed to get her launched. "I have to reconstruct," she said as Dad and their host walked away in conversation. "I stumbled on to that lighthouse exhibition by accident." When Dad was out of earshot, she lowered her voice. "I know this isn't the visit you expected, and I know your dad's preoccupied. But when this puffin census is done, he'll be able to relax with you."

The last person Joellen wanted to talk to about Dad was Abbie. Still, she was helpful. Even if she did lay it on too thick, she was a lot more aware than Dad. So instead of blowing her off, Joellen simply nodded.

"See," Abbie said, "I started out with birds and bird islands." She was running through options on the monitor. She spoke in an abstracted manner, as if she didn't really expect Joellen to listen. Then she straightened, and her voice brightened. "Okay, here's Fowlers now. There's a kind of overview. Want to see it?"

Joellen supposed so. Together they read the introduction, which began with a physical description of the island, eighty-six acres in extent, uninhabited until the first lighthouse was erected after the War of 1812, and of special interest because the island supported colonies of the Atlantic puffin and razorbill, these birds so exhaustively hunted that the populations had all but vanished.

"Where do you want to begin?" Abbie asked Joellen. "There's more about birds here and about storm petrels and terns on that small island."

"Is there a history, like a beginning, with the first lighthouse?"

Abbie searched but a moment before the information appeared. "A need had long been noted for a light on this outer island because of the many hazards to ships approaching the mainland. But so hostile were conditions in surrounding waters that it was not until 1821 that a lighthouse was built. In 1822 Samuel Orcutt was appointed Fowlers first lightkeeper."

"Orcutt Cove," Joellen exclaimed.

"You want to follow up with Orcutt Cove?"

Joellen shook her head. "I want to get to November 1848."

It took a moment for Abbie to figure out how to find this. "See," she said, "each topic is an index to more information. It may not be organized the way you expect." She clicked back to a more general menu. Then, returning to Fowlers, she ran through the 1820s. "Hey," she declared, "they even give you bits of the lightkeeper's logbook. Look at this entry for October thirty-first, 1829."

Joellen read: "Vilant storm. A saver gail Broak over headland."

"Looks like they had to rebuild the tower," Abbie observed. She passed through the years more slowly. "It's a different keeper now, 1835. And look, Joellen, look at these gales. November 1836 must have been a terrible month. The waves were so high they washed into the well and salted the water. Is this the sort of thing you're looking for?"

In spite of her eagerness to find out more about the events of November 1848, Joellen couldn't resist cruising the log with its record of ships passing and of unimaginable storms. "Sort of," she answered, figuring out that "chooner" probably meant schooner. As the log came up, she saw that in August 1838 Edwin Fossett became lightkeeper. "There!" she exclaimed.

"There, what?" asked Abbie. "That's 1838, not 1848."

"I know, but it's someone, I mean, it's a name I know." Her mind raced. Chris had mentioned an ancestor who was lightkeeper. Was the ancestor still keeper in 1848? "Let's slow down," Joellen suggested.

A moment later she reached out to grab the mouse from Abbie. "Hold it," she cried, staring at the log for January 27, 1839: "Lighthouse tore down by sea." Nothing more for two days, and then another brief entry: "Tree cut & trimmed and raised with beacon hoisted."

"Tough customer," Abbie murmured. "Just to survive must've taken guts."

"And he had a family there, too," Abbie said.

"How do you know?"

"I told you. I've heard about the Fossetts. They're still around. The guy who keeps sheep on Fowlers is a Fossett." She didn't exactly feel that she had to be secretive with Abbie, but what she and Chris had dug up belonged to both of them until they decided what to do with it. Still, it was hard to keep from blurting out what now looked likely: that it might have been Chris's ancestor who brought Patrick Healy and the other stranded people to the mainland.

"Let's see," Abbie murmured. "A new lighthouse was constructed in 1841, made of granite. That must be the one there now. Yes, here's a picture. Its lantern was upgraded in 1845 and a Fresnel lens, whatever that is, was installed in 1854, and so on. The light was automated in 1979." She had moved on through the years. Now she backed up to 1848. "I don't find anything . . ." Her words trailed off. "Are you sure about the date?"

Joellen nodded, her fingers itching to take over the keyboard and mouse.

Abbie shook her head. "Nothing here on Fowlers. It looks as though this exhibition cites only a few log entries as examples. You'd have to go to the source, to the archives, to cover a full year."

"Let me try," Joellen said.

"Okay. If you just wander around, you may bring something up. Sometimes it helps to back up and select a different link. This exhibition's got pictures as well as text and reproductions of letters and diaries." She rose and made room for Joellen. "Shall I hang around in case you need help?"

"I don't know. Can you just give me a little time, or are you going to the store?"

"I'll wait with the others awhile. Just call if you get stuck."

"Thanks," Joellen said, already switching back to the log for November 1848 and drawing a blank. Then a thought struck. Patrick Healy hadn't known the exact date. Maybe he was wrong about the month; maybe it was later than he thought. She called up December and at once was presented

151

with a new subject: "Missing Lightkeeper." Not quite what she was looking for. Or was it?

It began with a terse newspaper report of the grisly discovery near Ledgeport of four bodies cast ashore following a violent storm. Because no one was known to be missing, the authorities assumed that the victims had lost their lives at sea. They appeared to have put up a valiant struggle to save themselves, for they were tied to one another in an apparent effort to keep together, perhaps having lashed themselves to a part of the boat. One of the unfortunate victims was a woman, and one a boy. But the sea had taken such a toll on the bodies that even if someone had come forward to identify them, they were beyond recognition.

Joellen let this much sink in before moving on to a follow-up article that quoted from the same newspaper in early January 1849.

> During preparation for burial the only two bodies with intact feet were found to bear rope burns, indicating that the ankles were bound. Authorities now suspect foul play.
>
> No further information has come to light. Any unusual occurrence in this small, peaceful town is not likely to be overlooked, but there have been no reports of missing people, and there are no suspects. Inquiries have led to the discovery of one other curious event. Some two weeks before the bodies were found, Mr. Lyford Pierce, tacking inshore while heading for Ledgeport, observed a boat, empty and unattended, on the beach inside Popplestone Cove. The cove, which is long and narrow, shoals steeply. Any mariner with local knowledge would

avoid it, especially since Ledgeport Harbor is just three miles up the coast. Mr. Pierce recognized the boat as one belonging to Edwin Fossett, lightkeeper on Fowlers Island.

Although as far as he could tell there was no indication of distress, the sail ready to be hoisted and oars pulled back but in place as if departure were momentary, it was so unlikely a location for the lightkeeper to stop that on arrival in Ledgeport Mr. Pierce remarked on this sighting to the harbormaster. No one else had seen either the keeper or his boat.

After conducting some business on the waterfront, Mr. Pierce walked overland to see for himself that all was well. By the time he reached Popplestone Cove, the tide had risen and the boat was gone.

Authorities point out that the two incidents may be unrelated. However, they plan to question the lightkeeper as soon as it is possible to land on Fowlers.

The next entry in the computer was from an official inquiry dated January 18, 1849.

"You almost done?" asked Dad from the doorway. "We need to get a move on."

Joellen shook her head. "I can't. I'm in the middle of this."

"Well, try to wrap it up. We'll be back in civilization in a day or so."

"Please, Dad!"

"Honey, I'm glad this history thing grabs you. But

remember we're self-invited guests here. We can't take too much advantage of hospitality that—"

"John, let's get to the store." Abbie came up behind him. "I just found out they close early today." She was practically dragging Dad away with her. "Don't waste time reading everything now," she called to Joellen. "Just print out what you think you're going to want."

"Can I?" Joellen asked. "Can I do that?"

"No," Dad replied.

"Why not?" Abbie exclaimed. "We'll be grateful. We'll send a gift."

Dad didn't say no again. He just told Joellen to be ready to go in fifteen minutes. Joellen figured Abbie knew she was earning all sorts of points with her. Grinning, she ordered up the document. But there was too much. She had to specify pages or she would end up with reams of her host's paper. She supposed she didn't have to go much past the last reference to Fossett. But where was it?

Rolling through the next months, she caught tantalizing glimpses of the Fossett name. She printed out everything, including log entries, even though they seemed to be different. Then she turned up another item, a letter to the secretary of the treasury from Margaret Fossett. Did it have anything to do with Patrick Healy? Without taking time to read through it, she made a copy of that, too. Finally she came to a new section that stated simply that Albert Mossman took over his duties as keeper of Fowlers Island light on June 12, 1849.

When Dad called to her from the front door, she gathered up all the pages she had printed out, folded them, and shoved them into her knapsack. She could hardly wait to spread all this stuff out. She could hardly wait to show it to Chris.

27

Chris hunkered down to wait out the rain. Not at his exposed campsite but deep in the spruce woods where there was more protection from downpours. Still, everything he touched was saturated.

Even the sheep wanted to get out of the weather. They plodded past him, single file, until one got a whiff of him and wheeled around, starting a small stampede.

But it didn't last long. As soon as the milling ewes had reestablished contact with the right lambs, they moved on, a few of them casting him sidelong glances, full of mistrust that stopped short of outright fear.

He guessed they must have an even more protected spot where they bedded down during storms, but he didn't follow them. After all, it was their place. He would only drive them off.

It was dismal, this rain. He supposed he ought to be grateful that there was no wind with it, but gratitude didn't jibe with stupidity. For that's what he was—stupid. Stupid in the first place to talk himself into this week, and stupid in the second place to let Andy and Eric go away again without him. He wouldn't want to have to explain what he was doing here now, especially to Joellen.

He supposed she was comfortably nestled in the lighthouse room, maybe even in her sleeping bag to keep the chill off. She'd have a couple of candy bars to one side of her and some fruit and maybe a package of crackers on the other. And her notebook in her lap.

Probably she was wondering why he hadn't shown up to leave Patrick Healy's journal in the only completely dry place on the island. He hadn't had a chance to read it yet. He didn't dare take it out from under his foul-weather jacket.

In fact it was a pain keeping it wedged inside his belt. If he went across the island now, he could stow it in the lighthouse cellar and not have to worry about being careful. Besides, he could read it there. There wasn't anything else to do.

He waited for a letup between downpours and then headed for the shore path to avoid being deluged whenever he had to brush aside overhanging branches. As soon as he was out in the open, he felt less gloomy. Even under the leaden sky there was more light and a feeling of space. And it felt good just to have somewhere to go.

Figuring that this much rain would make the footing slippery, he gave the path above Dread Mans Cove a wide berth. Moments later, when he stumbled and the journal slid down a leg of his jeans, he scooped it up in something like a panic. If this mishap had occurred above the cove, the journal might have fallen onto one of those hopeless ledges. He clutched it against his body the rest of the way.

Not knowing where Joellen's father and his girlfriend were, Chris slowed and took plenty of time approaching the lighthouse. The horn moaned its two-tone warning out to sea. Overhead gulls mewed as they sailed on invisible waves.

Chris had to force himself not to call out to Joellen until he could be sure no one else was within earshot. From inside the cellar he heard no voices. But that didn't mean that Joellen was alone. He mounted the steps and then stopped.

Sometimes you can tell when a place is empty; it just feels that way. Well, they had probably gone back to the boat for lunch and then stayed there this afternoon. The cabin would be a lot warmer and drier than this unheated cylinder of stone. He'd choose the boat, too. Why not?

Before he settled down to read the journal, he went outside to check things out. If they were just about to come ashore again, he didn't want to be caught here unaware. The rain was heavier again, and he had to peer hard before he could admit to himself that the mooring was empty. Gone? How come? There must have been some kind of emergency.

He hurried back inside the cellar and shook out his foul-weather jacket before slinging it over a stair rail. Only then did it occur to him to look under the oil barrel. He saw with instant relief that Joellen's notebook was still there. She wouldn't have left it unless she was coming back. Put a lid on it, he told himself. He had no reason to care one way or another, except, he supposed, that after all the things they'd been doing together it seemed really strange to be completely alone again.

A slip of white paper protruded from her notebook. He guessed it was a message. As soon as he read that she was coming back soon, he had no trouble composing his feelings. This would be a good time to soak up the parts of Patrick Healy's journal he hadn't read yet. He could read undisturbed, without any of her comments to get in the way of his thinking. He needed to figure things out for himself.

He didn't realize until he was up in the room that he had carried her notebook with him. He set it down as he slid to the floor with his back against the wall. He opened the journal. But it was dark inside and hard to decipher the faded handwriting without so much as a flashlight. He struggled on for a couple of pages before closing the journal.

Idly, almost automatically, he picked up Joellen's notebook and opened it to the blank pages containing the keepsakes. He studied the picture for a while. But what could you tell from something solid black without detail? All of a sudden a word came into his head, something he must have learned from his aunt's shop. The word was *silhouette.* He felt almost smug being able to identify the type of portrait it was. Not that it helped, not that it brought him any closer to unraveling the mystery surrounding its survival in a hole in the ground for about 150 years.

He inserted it beside the hair and let the pages flip back, one after another, to good clear writing he could read. He was halfway down the page before he realized that he was reading Joellen's story, not a continuation of Patrick Healy's account.

It was weird. If she had written it before learning about Healy and the others, it was uncanny. If she had turned what they both had read in the journal into part of her story, it was so seamless that it couldn't possibly have come out any other way.

But it wasn't finished. She had simply come to an abrupt

halt. What was she waiting for? he wondered. Inspiration? Or did she expect to unearth some more evidence?

He turned back a page, absorbed as much by what she had crossed out as by what remained. The more he read, the more the story seemed to him like a fogbound vessel steering past rocks and ledges in search of a clear channel to some ultimate harbor. Then his perspective shifted as he backed and backed to the beginning with the girl left behind and island bound. Here at the start she was the nameless island girl from his grandad's lore. Only toward the last pages did she change and become a child with a name, become Flora.

But how could they be one and the same if Flora had once really lived?

28

It was one of those fogs that actually drip, as if the atmosphere were a gigantic sponge so saturated that water oozed from every air pocket. He was on that narrow sheep path above Dread Mans Cove. Someone was calling to him, but he knew it was a trick and he mustn't look. So he kept his eyes on the few inches of visible path before him, hoping to see the soft spot before he stepped on the unsupported turf and hurtled to the rocks below.

He had a feeling that if he kept his eyes open and properly focused, he couldn't miss the danger ahead. It was important not to let the voice distract him. "Not now," he tried to tell the person calling. "I'm looking for something." He found that he was following a puffin, silvery herring clasped in its red and yellow beak. All he had to do was catch the little bird and there would be a delicious meal of herring fried in butter.

The puffin stopped so short he almost fell over it, and

Joellen snapped, "Watch out, you jerk, you nearly stepped on the poor thing." Where had she come from?

The puffin stood in front of a mirror and darted its head from one side to the other as he had seen courting puffins do in the water. The mirror puffin grew frantic until the puffin Chris had been following strutted into the mirror and vanished. Chris stooped low to reach in after the bird and stubbed his fingers on the glass. He drew back and stared at what should have been his own reflection. Only it was that girl he had seen before, but this time with full face. Are you the ghost girl? he wanted to ask her, but he was afraid to speak out loud lest she retreat into the mirror like the puffin. Are you Flora? he wondered in spite of knowing this to be impossible.

"Goon," she said to him with Joellen's sharp-tongued inflection. "Can't you hear me?"

He stared up at her, seeing wild strands of hair like rock-weed fronds swirling on an incoming tide, seeing dark, unblinking eyes, seeing the mouth move like a video with the volume all the way down.

"I guess I fell," he mumbled, for why else would he be looking up at her now when at first she had seemed to come at him out of the mirror? "I was trying to focus," he explained. "It was in my way."

"What was in your way?" Joellen asked. "Focus on what?"

"On Flora, of course," he said. He pulled himself up. "I didn't know it was you."

"Then you haven't heard a word I said," she told him.

He shook his head. He guessed not. "What did you say?"

"That I found out everything, absolutely everything. I thought you weren't supposed to sleep inside."

"I didn't mean to. It just happened. Anyway, it doesn't matter. Do you know, I think I saw you before we met. I thought you were . . ."

"Who? Flora?"

He shook his head. "I didn't even know about Flora yet. I thought you were this, well, the ghost I mentioned."

"Oh, your grandfather's thing. That wouldn't be Flora, then," said Joellen, losing interest in this revelation. Squatting down, she zipped open her knapsack and drew out a sheaf of papers, which she dumped on the sleeping bag. "Wait till you read this stuff. It'll blow your mind."

"Why not Flora?" he asked.

Joellen shook her head. "I'm serious. I know a whole lot more now. I know she must not've died, because the keeper's wife would have buried her in the hole Patrick Healy dug. That's what she thought it was for. She didn't understand what he was telling her. It's all here. The police came to question the keeper. He never came back. He or his boat. She'd promised Patrick Healy that if the girl died, she would bury her in the grave she thought he'd prepared to make it easier for her because he was afraid Flora might die. And do you know who he was? I bet you can't guess."

"Who Patrick Healy was?"

"No, stupid, the keeper. Edwin Fossett. Your ancestor. Your great-great-great . . . something."

Chris gaped. He had sensed a kind of link between Flora and Joellen. But this was different, closer to home, if only he could figure out what it meant.

"Huh!" she exclaimed, gratified because Chris was finally struck dumb. "It's all in here," she went on, spreading the sheets of paper. "I printed out just about everything they had. And I was right about it being murder. Probably murder," she amended. "Anyway, a mystery no one ever solved. I guessed that."

"You guessed a lot of things," he retorted. "Only some were close."

There was a brief pause as she drew in a breath, then expelled it all at once. "You read my story!" she accused. "You read my private notebook."

"I didn't." He was so stunned by her violence, her sudden attack, that his denial came before he could think.

As soon as he had spoken, he knew it was a mistake. Only now he didn't want to admit that he had lied to her. "Anyhow, you knew I read some of it way back, and then you showed me what you wrote on that lined paper. So how come it's suddenly private?"

"It just is," she said. "I didn't write it for anybody to read."

"Isn't that what a story's for?" he asked. "To be read?"

"Not mine," she told him in no uncertain terms. "Especially the parts I've changed."

"I didn't know that," he said. "If I had, I would've just looked at the keepsake stuff. That's why I took the notebook up here. I didn't mean . . ." He words petered out. It was the closest he could come to an apology.

They sat quietly, Joellen's thoughts already veering away from her story and back on the track of the loose ends she had been pondering ever since she finished reading all the material she had printed out. For instance, the number of bodies seen didn't compute. But that could mean simply that some never washed ashore.

Last night she had been so caught up in all this that she hadn't thought about going to the lighthouse until after dark. By then, with the rain drumming on the cabin roof, it had just seemed natural to curl up under a blanket, warm and dry and drowsy.

Dad and Abbie had gone into the forward cabin, leaving Joellen to read and mull and read some more. Sometime during the night Dad must have come aft, because when she woke this morning, her flashlight was switched off and sticking up in the hammock. He had also opened the hatch a few inches, so the rain must have stopped by then.

Breakfast in the boat had gone pretty well. Joellen had made pancakes from a mix, and everyone had had seconds and then thirds. Then Dad made some comment about this history thing she was hooked on, about how it must be pretty hot stuff, at which Joellen had stiffened and gone silent. Abbie tried to smooth things over. She had remarked that while Joellen might look like her mother, there was also a lot of her father in her, too, like the way they both could shut out the world when they were involved in some consuming project. Dad, laughing, had responded that being obsessive was a family trait.

Then they had loaded up the dinghy and come ashore, Dad and Abbie going straight to work and Joellen practically flying to the lighthouse, never expecting that she would find Chris asleep inside.

"Don't you want to read it?" she asked him.

"I was thinking of food first," he said. "There's steamed mussels and clams back at my camp. At least I hope so." There was always a chance gulls had discovered his hidden supply and raided it.

"You could just eat some of my stuff," Joellen told him. "Since you slept inside last night. I mean, what difference does it make?"

Chris hadn't intended to spend the night here, so it

wasn't exactly cheating. "I've gone this far," he said, finally telling her the terms on which he was doing this survival stint. "I might as well hold on another couple of days. Then it's done."

Joellen shrugged. But she felt let down. If she woke up like this, real food wouldn't come first. She would be diving into the printouts to gobble up every morsel of information. She pulled a sheet from the spread of paper. "Listen to this," she urged as Chris stood up. "It's from the police report." She began to read: " 'On nine January 1849, the seas finally calm enough to effect a landing, the undersigned visited Fowlers Island to question Mr. Fossett, the lightkeeper.' See, they thought he'd be there, but he wasn't. Mrs. Fossett told them how weeks earlier he had left for the mainland, his own boat crowded with shipwrecked people. The exact date was in the log. The keeper had been concerned that his boat might be overloaded. But she never actually saw all of them. She guessed there were maybe six or seven people."

"Did she mention Mr. Hardison?" Chris asked.

"Not by name. Here's what the report says. 'The captain had been the only spokesman for the group. It was he who insisted that all the survivors be brought to the mainland together. It had something to do with discharging terms of a contract for which he could only then be paid. He was anxious not to meet with further delay, as other business pressed.' "

Chris said, "So who was killed?"

"Just wait," Joellen told him. "I'll get to that. Let me just finish this part. 'All had to be taken at once, except for a young girl, who was injured and ailing. Her mother was distraught at having to leave her but was reassured that the child would be in good hands until they returned for her.' "

"So then it wasn't Patrick Healy's group," Chris said. "Flora's mother wasn't there."

Joellen shook her head. "Don't you get it? Mrs. Fossett guessed Lucy was the mother. She didn't know. Just the way she guessed Patrick Healy must be the father."

Joellen read from the report: "'We asked Mrs. Fossett whether anything out of the ordinary had occurred at this time, to which she replied that the entire incident was out of the ordinary. But she did recall one other matter. A gentleman carried a child into her house. He spoke in haste and in accents that made him difficult to understand. She assumed he was so agitated because he feared that his child was close to death. He told Mrs. Fossett where he had dug a grave so that if what he feared came to pass, she would find everything in readiness. He regretted the trouble to the keeper's family but hoped that his foresight would ease their burden.'"

"That's not what he told her," Chris objected.

"No, but it's what she understood. The report shows this. Listen." Joellen read more. "'Mrs. Fossett was so occupied with caring for the child as well as her own family and the lights, which she and her eldest son, Amos, kept each night, that several days passed before she became concerned when the parents failed to return. She was not worried for her husband. Orders for supplies and the weather can detain him on the mainland. Once he was away for more than three weeks. He is an experienced seaman who would not risk setting out in a heavily laden boat unless confident of the sea and prospects for landing on this island. He knows the lights will be tended in his absence.'"

"Is that all?" Chris asked when Joellen fell silent.

"No, there's tons more. It's all here, including about the bodies."

166

"Whose? How many?"

"Four," she said. "Another showed up later."

"I'll come back to read it," he said. "I'm too hungry now." But he was hooked. Besides, he was afraid of returning to find the lighthouse cleaned out, Joellen gone. "Why don't you come with me? You can tell me more while I eat and dig another mess of clams."

She packed up all the papers. She wasn't about to risk a single page blowing away in the wind, which might happen if he started to read it on the beach.

29

Since Chris needed a moment alone for a pit stop, Joellen walked around the lighthouse. She gazed down over the rocks where, in 1839, the sea had risen in such a fury that it had torn down the previous lighthouse. It was impossible to visualize. Here she stood looking out at small gray waves churning in the aftermath of last night's rain. To live through such a tremendous storm seemed a triumph in itself. But Edwin Fossett had managed much more. He had erected a homemade beacon. Night after night he had kept it lighted and aloft to warn seafarers away from the dangers in these waters.

At the edge of the rounded rock that formed the outer-most limit of the island, she crouched down and peered into the cracks that age and weather had driven into the granite. Copper and silver-coated lamp reflectors had been hurled with such tremendous force that some had become deeply embedded in these fissures. Edwin Fossett had noted this in the log, adjusting and replacing his makeshift beacon so that the rocky headland glinted as though studded with tiny stars.

There was no sign of those bits of reflecting metal now, although she supposed some might still be there, covered by deposits from later storms.

"Looking for something?" Chris asked, coming up behind her.

She shook her head. She didn't want to get sidetracked about something that happened in 1839. She needed to put Chris in touch with all the clues dealing with 1848.

"What?" he said, looking where she had been looking.

She stood up. "Nothing," she told him, thinking that a man who would do what Edwin Fossett had done would never abandon his family and his duties. That's what Mrs. Fossett had believed, too. Even after the police had come from the mainland with news of bodies washed ashore and her husband's boat seen once in a deserted cove and seen no more. She couldn't shed light on the unidentified bodies, but she maintained her faith in her husband.

"What was the family story about the lightkeeper?" Joellen asked Chris. They had just come through the alders and were approaching Dread Mans Cove.

Where the sheep path forked, Chris led the way inland. "I'm not sure," he answered. "There's more than one version. They say he took off, either because of a woman or because he was afraid of being caught for something. It disgraced the family, which means the whole of Spars Island, since almost everyone in those days was related. I guess," Chris added, "it's the only case of lighthouse desertion on the Maine coast."

"Let's stay out of the woods," Joellen said. "I want to see Dread Mans Cove again." She wasn't sure why, except possibly because the name might have originally been Dead Man's. Could the keeper have returned to the island and somehow landed in the wrong place? But no, he knew this island perfectly, and he was an experienced seaman.

"The path's too close to the edge," Chris objected. "It'll be slippery after rain."

Joellen stopped. "I'm going that way anyhow. I'll meet you on the other side." She turned back and switched over to the path that edged the island.

Chris told himself it would serve her right if she took a tumble. But he knew that one wrong step could be her last, so he grudgingly followed.

"I'll be fine," she insisted when she realized he was coming after her.

"Yeah, right," was all he said, adding then, "I think I know a bit more about what can happen when it gets slimy around here than you do."

She kept her eyes on the path until she was able to look straight down into the center of the deep cove. "Do you think someone like Mr. Hardison would come in here?" she asked.

"No way," Chris replied. "No one with a grain of sense would try that. It's a one-way trip to hell."

"But if he wanted, say, to like dump a body?"

Chris shook his head. "It's a lot easier and safer to dump it at sea. Weighted, of course. But if you had the body on the island and could get it right here, this would be where to drop it. No one would be able to get close to it, right? And it wouldn't take the sea long to pulverize it on these rocks."

Joellen scowled. She was thinking hard. "Five bodies showed up far from here. We know there was the man and his two sons, Patrick and Lucy, Edwin Fossett, and Mr. Smythe and Mr. Hardison. That's eight people."

"What are you trying to say? And keep moving. I need my breakfast."

Joellen continued along the path. "At least one person must have come back to Fowlers Island," she said. For how else could a bracelet and a horn spoon have been removed from Patrick Healy's wrapped journal? "Probably the same person or people who pulled the keeper's boat up a few miles from Ledgeport Harbor. The police and others didn't think it was there for long because of the way it looked and because it could only have sailed or been rowed out before the tide left it stranded."

"They might've been wrong about it being the keeper's boat," Chris suggested.

"Except that it was the same day," Joellen argued, "the day he took everyone to Ledgeport. But wasn't seen there."

"I better read all your notes and stuff," Chris said. "It's not making sense. I don't see why you assume anyone came back here, especially since Mrs. Fossett doesn't seem to have mentioned anything like that."

"Of course not. She wouldn't have known. They wouldn't want her to know."

"They who?"

"I don't know, Chris. Mr. Hardison, I guess. Or Mr. Smythe. Or both."

Chris was able to catch up with her on this part of the path. They were walking side by side when he said, "No one came back. The only ones who would've wanted to were Edwin Fossett because he belonged here, and Patrick and Lucy Healy because they wanted to take Flora to a hospital. If she didn't die."

"If she'd died, Mrs. Fossett would have used the hole under the oak tree in the meadow because she thought it was supposed to be Flora's grave. Then she would've found Patrick's journal with the accusations, and the police wouldn't've been out here weeks later asking questions."

Chris was only momentarily silenced. Then he returned to his first position. "The point is no one came back."

Joellen shook her head. "Someone came who knew about the hole and dug up Patrick Healy's journal and took what they wanted, which was Flora's bracelet and the spoon."

In spite of his gnawing hunger, Chris stepped ahead and turned as if to block the way. Confronting her, he said, "Bracelet? Spoon? What are you talking about?" He had an uneasy feeling that she was somehow getting her own invented story mixed in with the facts they had uncovered.

"That Patrick Healy wrapped up with the journal. He told us about—"

"Wait a minute, Joellen. He didn't tell us anything. He told an unknown someone about his experience and his suspicions. That's all."

"Right. And that someone he didn't know turned out to be us. And even though it's too late for anyone who went through all that, we have to do what he hoped a reader like Mrs. Fossett would've done. We have to see that justice is done."

Chris almost laughed. She was so steamed up about all this that she thought it made a difference now. "You should meet my grandfather," he said. "You two have a lot in common."

"I want to," she retorted. "I want to ask him a whole bunch of questions."

172

Now Chris did laugh. "Good luck with him. He's a tough nut to crack."

"I thought you said he liked to talk about old family lore and this place."

Chris turned on his heel, leading the way and hurrying toward his campsite. He didn't imagine that he and Joellen would ever see eye to eye on all of this. But his curiosity was piqued by some of what she claimed. Was there really supposed to have been a bracelet and spoon with the journal? Why would anyone risk discovery to steal them from Patrick Healy's hiding place? Or had Joellen made them up for her story and now believed them real? He tried to recall whether she had mentioned them in her story. Maybe he had missed something. He had grown so drowsy reading in that darkening room. Besides, it was confusing sorting out which threads in her story she was keeping and which discarding.

The moment he clapped eyes on his heap of rockweed and saw that it was undisturbed, he fell on his knees, clawing off the insulating fronds to find the clams. He ate without pause, not trying to speak between mouthfuls, his greed overwhelming any inclination to share his bounty.

Joellen watched this feeding frenzy with revulsion. She suspected she would never want another clam, especially a cold one on a damp gray morning following pancakes and maple syrup and cocoa.

Chris polished off the clams and kept right on, eating mussels until he was gradually restored to a normal condition of mild hunger.

After a while yesterday's lunch didn't taste so good anymore.

30

While Chris picked mussels, Joellen concocted a plan. The more she had tried to convince him that at least one person had returned to Fowlers Island in order to steal the bracelet and spoon, the nuttier it seemed. Even if the bracelet were more valuable than it appeared to be, how would anyone else have been able to guess that? Patrick Healy had to have either told Mr. Smythe or shown it to him, and that seemed unlikely. Anyhow, the bracelet couldn't have looked like much if Flora was allowed to wear it on the ship, especially after she was sent to the coffin hold, where it could so easily have been taken from her.

Sitting with her back to the breeze, Joellen took out the sheaf of printouts. She was looking for some reference to Flora or even just a hint about what happened to her. But in all of Mrs. Fossett's replies to questions the police asked, the child was mentioned only once. Of course the exhibition included only a portion of the record. Maybe there would be something about her in the complete log. But Joellen had no access to these documents, and she wanted an answer now.

So when Chris dumped his final load of mussels and announced that he had to quit because the tide was coming up too fast, she blurted out her plan, which was to return to the hole where they had found the journal and look for stuff they might have missed. Naturally he couldn't know that she had been working it out in her mind and checking over the available information.

The look he gave her said everything. There he stood, drenched yet again, his stomach full for a change but slightly queasy, and silently willed her off the face of the earth. He shut his eyes for a moment. When he opened them, she was still there.

All of a sudden he knew what she reminded him of. She was like one of the orphan lambs they called bummers that had to be bottle-fed until they could eat on their own. The quick and clever ones soon learned to steal milk from other ewes, but they were always underfoot, always looking for a handout and tripping you up as you walked out to feed the home flock. Most visitors thought they were adorable, and Dad sensibly took whatever advantage of this he could, selling the bummers as bargains or sometimes even giving them away.

Chris would have given Joellen away if there were any takers. Speaking between clenched teeth, he said, "We fixed that hole. Remember? It was a big job."

"I know," Joellen told him. "I thought of that. We don't have to take the whole thing apart. All we have to do is uncover enough on top so I can slide down inside."

"You wouldn't be able to see," he said.

"I have the flashlight in my pack. And we know there were other things. If no one came and took them, they have to be there still."

"We don't know anything of the kind," Chris retorted. "You're inventing this."

"It's in Patrick Healy's journal. Didn't you read it?"

"Sure I did." He broke off. "No, I never got to it."

She jumped up. "Why not? What's the use of trying to figure this out if you don't know anything?"

"I couldn't read the damn thing in the rain. And when I finally took it to the lighthouse to read, it was too dark. I don't have a flashlight. I don't have a yacht that can take me to some convenient computer. So I don't know as much as you do. That's just how it is."

"Don't you care? You should, considering."

"Considering what?"

"That it's your family, Chris. Considering that Edwin Fossett was under suspicion, and still is. You can clear his name."

He shook his head. "Just because you were able to find out a few things doesn't mean we'll ever get all the answers."

"Which is why we have to try while we can. Come on, Chris," she pleaded. "Otherwise you're like a witness to a crime who pretends he didn't see anything because he doesn't want to get involved."

All in an instant the sun broke through the overcast cloud screen. It happened so suddenly it felt fake, as though someone had staged the return of light.

Chris wanted to take off his clothes and lay them out to dry. He wanted to soak up golden warmth as it overspread the beach until it was too hot to touch. Then he would dress in his sandy, salt-stiffened clothes, feeling at first as if he were incased in toast.

"Later," he said.

But she wouldn't be put off. "How much later? I can get started. You want to go back to the lighthouse and catch up on your reading? It's not just the journal; it's the end of the accusation, too. Here," she said, extracting her flashlight and a candy bar and stuffing the papers into her knapsack, "you can take this back with you in case you want to check something out, you know, between what Patrick Healy wrote and what Mrs. Fossett said. Then you can come when you're ready."

He found himself holding her knapsack, which he guessed amounted to a kind of agreement to her plan. "You better be careful," was all he could think of to say.

"Well," she told him breezily, "if I get stuck like that old sheep, I'm sure you'll rescue me."

He could think of a number of retorts, but he kept his mouth shut. They parted there on the foreshore, Joellen striding directly into the woods and Chris heading for the coastal route in the hope of contact with the sun. By now he had a headache and a definite stomach gripe. With a huge effort of mind over matter, he managed to hold on to his breakfast until just before Dread Mans Cove. He lost it hanging his head over rocks where, sooner or later, the sea would clean up after him.

Afterward he was so chilled that he rummaged in Joellen's pack and found a down vest that easily fitted him. It crossed his mind that this was against the rules. It also crossed his mind that he didn't care. He considered detouring in search of some spruce sap to take the awful taste from his mouth, but he couldn't be bothered. He just put one foot in front of the other, figuring that he would eventually reach the lighthouse, where he might give himself a few minutes under Joellen's sleeping bag before taking up the homework she had assigned him.

"Hello?"

Chris stopped in his tracks. He had completely forgotten to look before approaching. And now a man and a woman stood facing him. Of course. Sooner or later it was bound to happen.

"Hello," he replied.

"I didn't know anyone else was here," Joellen's father said. "Didn't see a boat. You're aware, aren't you, that this area is off-limits?"

Heat finally stirred and began to spread through Chris's body. These people from away, he thought, they really did act like they owned the whole Maine coast. He said, "My father keeps sheep on this island," and then he didn't dare go on. He was afraid he'd throw up again.

"Oh, yes," Joellen's father replied. "Fossett. We've spoken."

Chris nodded.

Then Joellen's father noticed the knapsack. "That's my daughter's!" he exclaimed. "What's going on here?"

Chris said, "I'm taking it to the lighthouse for her."

"Where is she?" He stepped toward Chris, almost menacingly. "Where's Josie?"

Chris was fed up. Where did this guy get off playing the heavy with him? "Digging," Chris said. "Hunting."

"What are you talking about?"

"Ask her," Chris said in a tone meant to say a lot more.

"Now you listen here—" Joellen's father began.

"John." The woman, Abbie, put a hand on his sleeve.

Then she spoke to Chris. "Are you into this lighthouse history, too?"

Chris nodded, responding to her friendly voice. "Joellen helped me with a sheep that was in trouble, and that led to finding something that we're trying to make sense of."

"There," she said, removing her hand from Joellen's father's arm. "Perfectly straightforward."

"Except that this young man's been in the drink," he declared, staring at Chris's wet clothes and apparently not recognizing the vest.

Chris didn't think he had to supply this guy with an explanation.

"Is Joellen wet, too?" Abbie asked.

"No," Chris said. Then he added, because he couldn't resist needling Joellen's old man, "At least she was dry when I last saw her."

"How long ago was that?"

Chris shrugged. "Twenty minutes. Half an hour maybe." He moved as though to walk past the couple and then turned to say, "She's got a candy bar. Do you want me to take her some lunch?"

Abbie said that would be great. Joellen's father didn't look too happy about the situation, but he was clearly backing down from his hostile stance.

"Tell her not to be late this afternoon," he said to Chris, who was on his way to the lighthouse.

Chris deposited the knapsack beside Joellen's sleeping bag and went down to the cellar to get the journal. He hesitated. He really didn't feel like reading it now. But he might as well have it on hand for later on. Then he wouldn't have to return for it and risk coming up against Joellen's father, who thought he was God or something.

Abbie met Chris coming out of the bulkhead. She handed him a sandwich in a plastic bag. "Would you like one, too?" she asked. "We have plenty."

He wasn't even tempted. But he went out of his way to be polite and accepted two bananas to go with the sandwich just because, as she said, he might feel like one later on.

31

It was darker and messier than Joellen had expected beneath the crude scaffolding and cover, but surprisingly dry. She was determined to locate the missing bracelet and spoon before the skeptical Chris joined her.

When she failed to unearth anything but root tendrils around the hole where they had discovered the oilskin-wrapped journal, she started to grope through the loose subsoil and pebbles and spruce branches that lined the floor of the pit. Of course that meant crawling around on sheep droppings as well. At least the smell would discourage Dad from trying to get her to stay with them in the boat again. She was coming closer to figuring out the end of her story. She needed to be alone to finish it.

"Joellen? Joellen, are you there?"

"Yes," she called up to Chris. "I thought you were going to read for a while. Don't you want to get clued in?"

"I couldn't. I met your dad and Abbie. I brought your lunch." He sounded odd, his tone sort of flat.

"Was there trouble?"

Chris shook his head. He folded his arms across his stomach and braced himself against the nausea that surged up in him.

"Chris? What happened?"

He gasped. He couldn't speak until the assault subsided. Then he said, "Nothing important. Did you find anything?"

"I'm giving up down here. Do you want to look?"

"No. Come on out." The canopy shifted slightly. "Watch it," he warned.

She had pulled aside just enough of the covering to slither wormlike into the pit. But she couldn't climb out without a bigger opening, which meant dislodging some of the big branches. She reached up toward the hole she had made and asked him if he thought he could pull her out. He grunted something she couldn't understand, but a moment later he was extending his hands down to hers.

"You'll have to like climb up the side," he said. He clutched her wrists, his grip both icy and damp.

For a moment she thought her arms would come off. Then she found shallow toeholds that gave her a bit of boost.

Once during the climb he said, "Wait," in a strangled tone. She realized that he had to rise from a kneeling position. He let go of one wrist, then grabbed it again and hauled with renewed strength and the advantage of height. When she was more than half out, she was able to squirm the rest of the way.

She lay on the ground a moment, then rolled over and sat up. She began to pick off the debris that clung to her clothes and hair."I can patch that hole," she said. "All the main pieces are still there. It'll be just as safe as before."

When he didn't respond, she looked up to see beads of sweat standing out on his face. Laughing, she said, "I didn't know I was that big of a load."

He shook his head. Still no words came.

She scrambled to her feet. "Are you all right?" she asked.

He shook his head and again said, "Wait." He sank down, bowed his head, and wrapped his arms around himself. He felt breathless and hot and chilled all at the same time. Damn, he thought. Damn.

Joellen watched him for a moment. Then she went to work to cover the hole she had made. She had to walk into the woods a ways to find strong branches without any rot in them.

When she returned with her haul, he looked more relaxed. It was a relief to see that he wasn't seriously injured. She would feel awful if he had wrenched something really badly while he was helping her.

After she had covered the hole, she crawled over and sat beside him. She wasn't sure what should be done next.

Finally he said, very quietly, "I think some of my . . . breakfast was bad." He couldn't bring himself to say the words *mussels or clams.*

"Oh." He could be really sick. He might need a doctor. He should get warmed up. "You can't stay here," she said.

He nodded but made no effort to stand up or move. It was weird being so shaky that he was willing to let Joellen take charge.

"Can you walk to the lighthouse?" she asked him.

"I guess." He grinned weakly. "Unless you're offering to carry me."

"Seriously. I can get my father."

"No way," he managed to say with some vigor.

"Well, let's go then. There's a thermos of plain tea and one of sweet tea with the lunch stuff. Do you think you could drink some?"

He nodded.

"Chris," she said to him, "you better let my dad take you to Ledgeport."

He shook his head. "I'll be all right." He stood up and started off in the wrong direction.

"No," she cried. "Where are you going?"

"Have to get my stuff," he told her.

"I'll get it," she said. "You start for the lighthouse, and I'll catch up."

He turned. The woods were too dark. He longed to lie down and be warm. He might get to the shore path and just rest there in the sun.

"Stay away from Dread Mans Cove," she told him.

He nodded, heading for the light. Then he said, "I just went. Remember? I was there. I'm fine." But he knew that he wasn't. He had never felt like this before. Trudging on, he realized that she was behind him. He stopped. "What about my stuff?" he asked thickly.

"I'll go back for it," she promised. "I don't want to leave you alone here."

He tried to laugh her off, but she wouldn't be budged. The bummer lamb on his tracks again. He shrugged and walked on.

Twice he had to stop for dry heaves. Joellen was horrified. He sounded as though his insides were being torn out. She felt helpless and stupid. And scared. After the second episode he rested awhile.

"Talk," he finally ordered.

"What about?" she asked, wondering whether she should run ahead to get Dad.

"You know. Your favorite subject."

Was he serious? He wanted her to talk about Patrick Healy and Flora? She would have to think of something not crucial, something he didn't need to know. She searched her memory and came up with nothing. It was all she had thought about for days, and now she was blank.

"Go on," Chris said as if she were in the middle of a story.

"Shouldn't we keep going?" she asked, wondering how many more times he would have to stop like this.

"In a minute," he said. "Tell me about Mrs. Fossett. What happened to her?"

"She stayed on here for months until the new keeper came. That was in June, I think, or July. She wanted the job. She wrote a letter to the secretary of the treasury, who was the person who appointed lightkeepers. She was turned down because Fossetts were considered untrustworthy after her husband deserted."

Joellen paused to let Chris comment. When he didn't speak, she continued. "It seems so unfair. She was a good keeper. She was a better speller than her husband, by the way. You can see that in her log entries, which mention staying up all night to trim the wicks and having trouble with the summer oil in the cold weather and carrying it up all those steps. She cleaned the lamps every morning to be ready for each night. And once she and her son Amos rescued some people and kept them much longer than when they had provided food for Patrick Healy and those others. She was so short of supplies by the time a boat came and could take them off that all they had to eat were eggs and cornmeal mush."

With those last words, Chris could feel his stomach begin to churn again. He clenched his jaws.

"Sorry. I should've left that out."

"And nothing more about Flora?"

"The log's about keeping the light. Mrs. Fossett mentioned the food because the keeper was supposed to be paid for something like that. I don't think she ever was. And she had to sell almost all her farm stock to the new keeper because she couldn't take much with her. She and her family went to live with her sister on Coombes."

Chris nodded. That jibed with family history. While some Fossetts had stayed on Coombes and worked in the quarry and polishing mill, Grandad's side had moved to Spars to work in the fish-canning factories. Grandad had an old photograph of children cutting and boning fish at a table in front of a drying yard. Grandad claimed that he was one of the small boys in the foreground, his back to the camera, which showed row upon row of wire racks laden with fish stretching all the way to the canning shed. Chris used to think that if he could turn the picture over to see the kid's face, he would be able to see if Grandad was telling the truth about himself.

As if the truth were just beyond reach, on the other side of an old snapshot.

He got to his feet again. He said, "Listen, I'm all right now. I can make it by myself."

He did sound more like himself. But she didn't trust the situation. There was no telling where he might be when another wave of nausea knocked him over. She said, "Don't worry. It won't take me long to bring your sleeping bag and knapsack to you."

"I'm not worried about them. I'm just trying to save you one more round trip."

"So let's go," she told him firmly.

On the last leg of the way he managed not to stop. But by the time they pressed through the alders and the lighthouse was in sight, he was drenched with sweat. He just gritted his teeth and forced himself to keep going because he was almost there.

He made it all the way, staggering under a weight that seemed to close over his head, pressing almost unbearably, making his eyes tear as if he were crying.

Joellen brought him a thermos and poured out tea. "Get in my sleeping bag," she ordered.

He couldn't manage that. He just crawled underneath and pulled it up to his chin.

She handed him the cup, then helped him hold it.

"Watch out," he warned. "You'll be in range if it doesn't stay down."

"Drink," she said, wondering how to get him down the ladder to the dinghy. "This wasn't the way it was supposed to come out," she murmured, and then realized that she had spoken thoughts that she meant to keep to herself.

"Can say that again," he responded. He was afraid of taking even tea into his mouth. He took a sip. It wasn't hot, but it was warm still and very sweet. He sipped some more, and then leaned back against the wall.

She left the cup beside him and ran outdoors to get her father. She hoped she didn't have too far to shout. Any ruckus would make him furious. But she found him near the top of the cliff, loosening the bolts that held down one of the mirrors. She told him that Chris Fossett was sick and that it might be food poisoning. Really sick, she emphasized when Dad gave her a look of disgust.

"Where's his father? I thought he was there on the other side of the island."

Abbie joined them as Joellen explained that Mr. and Mrs. Fossett were in New Zealand looking at sheep.

Dad said, "They could've stayed home to do that," but he walked rapidly toward the lighthouse. She couldn't tell whether his speed reflected urgency or irritation.

The moment he clapped eyes on Chris, his whole manner changed. First he felt Chris's pulse. Then he asked him what he had eaten and when. Joellen supplied the answers.

"What possessed him?" Dad exclaimed. "Who's with him?"

"It's a survival thing," Joellen said. "He was here alone. On purpose."

Dad groaned. "Who's responsible for you?" he asked Chris.

"Grandfather," Chris answered. "Don't . . . This place freaks him out. Don't call him or anything. He'll go ballistic."

After Chris drank a little more tea, Dad decided to go to the boat to call a doctor on the radiophone.

"I'll stay here," Joellen said.

"My stuff," Chris mumbled.

"Later, Chris. I promise."

"If you want to get his things, I'll keep an eye on him," Abbie offered.

Joellen shook her head. She was in too much of a stew to think about anything as trivial as Chris's sleeping bag, which was probably still wet anyhow. "If you go with Dad," she said to Abbie, "you can be putting things together, food and stuff to bring back, while Dad's getting advice. It'll be quicker."

This brought a wan smile across Chris's sallow face.

"What?" she snapped as Abbie took off after Dad.

Chris closed his eyes. "Watching you operate . . ." He left the rest of the comment hanging between them.

32

It was a full-scale invasion of the lighthouse. Not only did Dad insist on their all spending the night with Chris, but he filled the room with bags of clothes and blankets and sleeping bags, his Coleman stove, pots, water jugs, and every manner of food that the doctor he consulted suggested that Chris might try at various stages of recovery.

At first Chris could keep nothing down but tea. Joellen's father didn't seem too worried about that. He would go back to the boat to speak to the doctor again just before nine that night. In the meantime, he said, the main objective was to deal with Chris's dehydration. As long as Chris kept drinking tea or warm sugared water, he would be ahead of the game. That meant they wouldn't have to call for extreme measures like an emergency rescue.

"I'd rather die," Chris had mumbled when Joellen's father had spelled it all out.

"That would be the alternative," Joellen's father had told him. "But it doesn't look as though it'll come to either. Our goal is to get you aboard tomorrow and to Ledgeport. That'll depend on your getting strong enough to make it to the boat. Also the weather. It should be fair, but they're forecasting a stiff breeze out of the northwest. We'll just have to wait and see."

When they were outdoors, Joellen's father filled her in. The doctor had suspected that polluted water might be behind Chris's violent reaction to the shellfish, which were unlikely to have gone bad under the recent cool, rainy conditions. Unless, of course, he had covered them when they were still hot from being on the fire. Joellen's dad was to check Chris frequently for the onset of other symptoms. Even so, Dad said, what happened should be taken seriously. If Chris had been alone when he sickened, he might not have made it.

"I am taking it seriously," Joellen said. "I did."

Dad nodded. "I know. You kept your head." He paused. "You've gotten to know him some?"

"Sort of."

"Do you know what's going on with the grandfather?"

"A little. Not much."

"Well?" he prompted.

"His grandfather's like superstitious about Fowlers Island." Joellen couldn't help feeling that she was betraying Chris's confidences. "Like it's kind of haunted. Not just his grandfather, but others, old-timers, half believe Fowlers is jinxed, especially for the Fossett family. You know all the stuff I've been learning about? It looks like there's something real behind it. Only they don't know that. They just have this feeling based on memories that are only partly right." She fell silent. How could she bring up the whole story now when Dad was so riled about being interrupted just as he wrapped up this phase of his work here?

Dad said, "You should've told me about Chris being here."

"Why?" she demanded. "What difference did it make to you? He was minding his own business."

"Everything on this island is my business, at least until August when the puffins leave."

Joellen said, "That pretty much sums up the way Chris and his dad feel about you and your project. They and their sheep were here first."

Instead of lecturing or arguing, Dad just nodded. It was time to check in with the boy again.

"Do you have to keep waking him up?" Joellen asked as her father bent over Chris and spoke his name.

"Absolutely. Chris?" Dad's voice filled the room. "Tea time, Chris."

Chris moaned and then opened his eyes, only to squeeze them shut at once. Abbie drew close. Keeping her voice low, she explained that Dad was looking for changes. If the Coast Guard had to come for Chris, it would be about the worst thing imaginable, since a helicopter landing here could devastate the puffin project's first nesting. Dad had to be very careful not to misread the situation.

"Light bother you?" Dad asked, his flashlight poised over Chris's face.

Chris turned his head aside. "Yup."

"Need to pee?"

"No."

Dad propped his own rolled sleeping bag behind Chris. "Feel like trying some chicken broth?

Chris shook his head. He took the mug of tea, his hands trembling, but he was able to steady it on his own. He took small gulps, as if drinking made him breathless. Then he leaned his head against the wall. He figured his head must be getting back to normal, but he didn't feel like putting it to a rougher test. The important thing was to keep as still as possible.

"Bellyache?" Joellen's old man asked. "Do you feel bloated?"

"No." Well, yes, his head had felt bloated, but it was shrinking down to size now.

Joellen's old man actually reached down inside the sleeping bag and probed around like a doctor. Chris would have told him to get his hand the hell off his stomach if it didn't take so much energy to speak.

"Progress," declared the phony doctor. "Less tightness than before. Do you want to sit up for a while?"

Chris wanted not to move. The questions wore him out. He wished they'd all go away and leave him in peace.

At least Joellen had the sense to suggest that they eat their supper outdoors to keep the food smells away from Chris. Maybe if he fell asleep before they came back inside, they'd let him be.

But he woke up on his own. He was a bit more alert now. Whatever bug or poison had overwhelmed him earlier was beginning to let go. He shrugged off a blanket that was spread on top of the sleeping bag. Whose? he wondered. He reached for the half-empty mug of tea and drank it all down.

By the time Joellen's dad and Abbie went back to the boat for the evening call to the real doctor, Chris had had a few swallows of broth and a spoonful of Abbie's yogurt. His stomach started to grumble.

"You going, too?" he asked Joellen.

"Just down to get my notebook." She returned in a minute or so, planning to look it over while Chris slept and the others were away.

But Chris wasn't sleeping. "Sorry," he said. "Your old man pissed?"

"I don't know. He was almost done now anyhow. I think he was scared you might, you know, be not all right."

"You mean that I'd croak?"

She nodded.

"Couldn't do that," he said. "It would've finished Grandad."

"My dad was asking about him," Joellen said. "I wasn't able to tell him much."

Chris shifted down onto his side and propped his nearly normal head on his hand. "It's hard to tell what parts of Grandad's stories are true."

"You've told me that."

"When he was three or four years old, there was a family excursion to Fowlers Island. His grandmother tried to stop them going. She said it would be the death of them. It was."

"What do you mean? Are you okay talking this much?"

"I guess." He waited a moment before going on. "Grandad's grandmother refused to go with the others. She saw them off, though. She had Grandad by the hand and wouldn't let him down to them in the boat. As it pushed off, it had to turn. It went counterclockwise. That was an omen, turning against the course of the sun, and she knew for sure that they were doomed."

"What happened?"

"Grandad says there were witnesses, another boat along on the outing at the lighthouse. They got caught by this surge, an underground swell straight off the Atlantic. Swamped the one boat. Grandad's mother and older brother drowned. His father tried to save them, barely made it himself, and never fully recovered. Sounds like his lungs were shot. He died a few years later. So Grandad's grandmother raised him up. He said she had a will of iron. She's the one that taught him out of that schoolbook he still has. Taught him everything."

In the aftermath of this account Joellen could hear Chris's quick, shallow breaths.

"Taught him to be superstitious?" Joellen finally asked.

"Seems like it. About the island girl for sure. That lesson stuck with him all his life. He even brought it up when I told him where I'd be this week. Bad luck, he said. No Fossett's ever got the better of her."

"But you and your dad come here for the sheep," Joellen reminded him.

"Yup. And Grandad says he always holds his breath till we're safe home."

"Did you ever ask him who the girl was? How his grandmother knew about her?"

"According to what his grandmother said, the girl was—" Chris broke off.

"Was left there?" Joellen finished for him.

A shudder ran through him. "Sad and fierce," he whispered.

"Flora," said Joellen quietly. Almost everything was sliding into place. "If only we could find out what happened to her."

He thought a moment. "It could describe . . . other people," he suggested.

"What others? Do you have anyone else in mind?"

Chris closed his eyes. All this talking had left him drained but clearheaded. "You," he said.

Before she could think of a retort, he was sound asleep.

33

The day was blustery, but so bright you could see every rock and ledge, black and shiny, like seals nosing up for air. It was almost noon when Chris had to go out. Joellen's father helped him on the stairs and then didn't want to let him out of his sight.

"I'm all right," Chris said, meaning he wanted some privacy.

Joellen's father backed off. But as soon as Chris seemed to be heading away, Joellen's father called out sharply. Chris was to wait inside until they were ready to get him down to the boat.

Chris squinted against the dazzling light. "I have to look for something." There was still a dull ache behind his eyes. He didn't want to explain what he was after in case he was wrong. For the same reason he hadn't said anything to Joellen.

The recollection had surfaced just as he awoke. There was something about the twisted sleeping bag that brought back that restless night he had spent in the cellar hole. He had felt stifled and bound then, too. He had struggled to free himself until in his clumsiness he had thrust off the whole awkward covering. There had been no reason to be even slightly curious about the thing that clattered to the stony ground. A circle of heavy-gauge wire, he had thought at the time, if not the coil from a bedspring. Either was a good bet in a place where a house had once stood and a garden had probably been fenced to keep sheep out.

But he couldn't leave the island now without seeing the thing that he had tossed aside. If it was still there.

According to what Joellen had told him, there should have been two things, a spoon as well as a bracelet. Maybe the spoon had fallen out of the box-shaped oilskin earlier. A metal spoon should have made even more of a clatter unless it had landed on something soft like moss.

"Chris!" Joellen's father called.

"Coming," Chris answered. "In a minute." It was weird being so unsteady that just leaning over made him dizzy. If he didn't plant his feet with exaggerated care, he listed like some leaky derelict of a boat.

If only Joellen were still here to keep her father out of his face. But she had already started across the island and would stay there until Andy and Eric showed up. Low tide. That was the meeting time they had agreed on. She would hand them his stuff and tell them that he would be taken back on her father's sloop. Her dad had insisted that she set them straight and let them know he had been sick. "No more games," he had instructed the two of them.

Joellen had begun to protest. It wasn't her game. But now

that the crisis was dealt with and the adjustments made to get Chris home, her dad was on edge and in a blaming mood.

Chris had no trouble finding the exact spot where he had slept. It was near the corner where the two remaining foundation walls joined. He had slung the thing at that wall. It might have bounced a bit.

Chris didn't realize until he actually saw the thing that he had been prepared to find a different-looking object. A bracelet should be silver or gold, something like that. Even if it was tarnished, wouldn't it have an ornamental appearance?

This was, at first glance, so much like his first guess about its being a bedspring coil that for a moment he thought he had guessed right. He couldn't stoop to pick it up. He had to brace himself against the wall and ease himself down to his knees. Once he had the circlet in his hand, he concentrated on getting onto his feet again. The effort was unnerving. It brought back a trace of nausea.

Finally, standing and swaying a little, he turned his back to the sun for a real look at what was in his hand. It was some kind of discolored wire, braided, surprisingly heavy. Not quite a full circle. One end was tapered like a lizard's tail. The other end, more blunted, gave an impression of a flattened, featureless head.

"Chris," said Joellen's father, standing on the ruined wall and blocking the direct sun, "I'm glad you're better. But you're not to fool around, at least on my time."

Chris stuffed the bracelet into his pocket. Looking up without having to squint, he nodded. It was probably not a good idea for Joellen's father to discover how crummy he still felt.

He made a huge effort to walk with apparent ease and

without holding his arms out for balance. Something, a stick from the sound of it, or maybe a bone, snapped underfoot and then crunched. Fighting nausea and dizziness, he didn't dare shift his gaze. Anyway, it wasn't anything metallic that might be a spoon, so he didn't need to examine it.

What mattered now was getting up the slope somehow. After that he would have to tackle the lighthouse stairs.

34

The sea darkened before Joellen's eyes. It wasn't a menacing darkness. Despite all the whitecaps that pranced and tossed their heads of spume, there was a glittering freshness in this deep blue wildness.

The seals on the outlying ledge seemed to grow restless even though they had plenty of haul-out space with the tide this low. Watching them, she suddenly recalled the first image she had conjured up of shipwrecked survivors stranded on a ledge, not seals that could swim away, but people doomed as the water rose and engulfed them. Was that what had happened to Mr. Hardison's victims? She wished that she had never invented that scene. She had to remind herself that imagining it did not cause what had happened to those real people in December 1848.

A raft of eider ducks rode waves that seemed to thrust them back as they swam toward shore. The ducks coasted and plunged in the confusion of wind against the tide. So it had turned, thought Joellen. She supposed the ducks took all the wind shifts and tide changes in stride. A sea duck wouldn't think of its home as menacing or fresh. It was just there, and so were they.

She picked up Chris's gear and moved it closer to the water. When his friends appeared, any moment now, she would call them in close and then carry everything at once if she could. She looked over the rocks at either end of the beach, wondering which would be the best to clamber out on. Probably Andy or Eric would be able to tell the safest approach for making contact with someone on shore.

Very likely Mr. Hardison had made such a judgment in attempting to land here one hundred and fifty years ago. Possibly at that point he had no evil intentions beyond taking his victims for an expensive ride, which was a kind of robbery, and leaving them to fend for themselves. She supposed that the loss of his boat had turned everything upside down for him. Without a vessel he couldn't carry on his cruel traffic in human lives. So he had to rewrite the rules of his game.

She wondered whether Mr. Smythe had been in on the plan to take over the lightkeeper's boat. Could Mr. Hardison have carried it out alone? Maybe Mr. Smythe helped without realizing it and never caught on until it was too late. Mr. Smythe liked Patrick Healy. How could he have turned on him?

Or was Mr. Smythe just another witness by then? If so, he, too, would have become a victim like the lightkeeper, Edwin Fossett. After Mr. Hardison got rid of them all, did he go on smuggling more desperate and unsuspecting passengers from the coffin boats? What kind of person could use people that way and dispose of them afterward?

There was so much she would never know. Still, in time she might learn something more. Or had she and Chris already stumbled on the heart of Flora's story?

The brisk wind carried a memory of winter cold. Joellen shivered. How could anyone know what Flora had endured after months on the ship where her mother had died? She must have been beyond cold in that November storm that cast her broken on this shore. And then? Then finally warmth and nourishment. But never again to see a face from her past or hear a familiar voice from home. And never to know why she had been left to wait in vain for rescue and reunion.

This was a story that needed to be told. It had seemed to Joellen, at least for a while, that she had been writing it. But Flora wasn't a nameless character whose life could be shaped to suit someone else's sense of drama the way the island girl had been taken over by those who made her a ghost. Even if Joellen could get closer to the truth, she knew that she would not write it. Because, she now realized, it had already been told. Flora had turned this part of her life into story, making of it what she needed.

Had she kept it to herself, for herself? That seemed likely, at least for a while. Then later, as the years passed, the story of the island girl must have taken on a life of its own, maybe as Flora's children grew old enough to listen to it. And that would have been long before she told her grandson, who was Chris's grandad, about the child who haunted Fowler's lonely headland.

Joellen was amazed that she had been so slow to see this. Understanding seeped into her like a rising tide, its fullness lifting her out of her time.

She saw the boat bounce into view without hearing the engine. It felt eerie, dreamlike. Even knowing that the boys were bucking an offshore wind couldn't dispel a sense of unreality, especially when she noticed they were not alone. Her mind couldn't resist the image that had already become so fixed in her imagination, an image of that other boat in that other time in the moments before it foundered on some of these very rocks.

For a moment she simply stared. It was as if in the next instant details of the picture would materialize. Instead of these two boys and the man between them, the others would appear, the ones without names along with Patrick Healy and Lucy and Flora, and of course Mr. Hardison and Mr. Smythe. She almost turned inland to glance back through time to when a single oak tree stood in open meadowland not far from this shore.

35

The boat scattered the raft of ducks.
Joellen couldn't help comparing the ease with which they
bobbed and coasted, yielding to the boat, with the boat itself,
bucking and slamming each wave. When it drew closer,
the two boys stood. The man between them was hunkered
down, no doubt drenched from the rough ride. From the
look of him she guessed he was Chris's grandad.

She picked up Chris's gear and headed out to meet them.
When the boat was within a few feet of a rock she thought
she could get to, she started to clamber across to it. But the
going was slippery. Everything she carried threw her off-
balance.

One of the boys looped a line around a smaller rock but
didn't make it fast. "Where's Chris?" he shouted.

Knowing Chris hadn't wanted to alarm his grandad, she
had to pick words that would downplay the situation. "He's

all right," she started to say. "But he got sick yesterday. My father will bring him to Ledgeport. He wanted me to give you his stuff." She raised the sleeping bag to toss it to the boy in the stern. Although the boat was pitching and swinging from the line, the old man stood up, grabbed the gunwale, and leaned out toward her. It was he who took the hit, the sleeping bag knocking him backward.

"I'm sorry," she said. "Is he all right?"

The boy in the stern tried to help the man onto a thwart, but he shook off the boy and reared up to face Joellen.

Thank God, she thought. Not hurt. He wasn't likely to have been hurt by a mere sleeping bag, but he might have struck something when he fell down inside the boat.

"Sorry," she told him. Would she have to ask him to get out of the way of the knapsack? She had tied the gallon jug to it with the end of the coiled rope. It would be a more awkward throw.

"Where's Chris?" the old man demanded, fixing her with the most intense look she had ever seen. "What have you done?"

"I told you. He got sick. He's fine. He will be, I mean." Then she added, "He didn't expect you to come."

One boy said, "He made us bring him. See, Wednesday when we checked on Chris, he told us there was a girl here. We thought he was kidding. But he said she was at the lighthouse, off a boat on the mooring. So when we left him, we went around that way. We didn't see a boat or anyone. We like passed the joke on to Mr. Fossett. We told him Chris was fine but was seeing a girl that wasn't there. The old-timers, they have this like dumb idea about a ghost girl."

"I know," Joellen said. "I know about that." She turned to Chris's grandad. "Chris got sick on clams or water or something. No one did it to him. I have to get back now.

We were just waiting for Andy and Eric to tell them what happened to him."

"What happened?" the old man demanded. "I want to see him."

"I just said. You'll see him in Ledgeport in a few hours." Trying to hand over the knapsack rather than risk throwing it, she slithered down the rock, her sneakered feet and then her ankles submerged and still sliding. While the boy in the stern clutched the gear, she leaned out to grab the boat and steady herself.

Chris's grandad clamped his hands down over hers. She thought he was going to try to pull her up the way Chris had pulled her from the pit. She was stretched full length, still trying to keep the rest of herself out of the water. But the boat kept tugging her from her underwater perch. She needed to thrust herself back. "Let go," she said, gasping as the cold bit into her.

He did let go, but only to take hold of her shoulders. His fingers dug through her jacket in a powerful grip. She lost her footing entirely and for an instant was caught in sheer terror. Instead of holding on to the gunwale, she found herself fighting to break free. It was senseless and futile, but she couldn't help it.

The struggle, if that was what it was, lasted only a few seconds before the boy in the stern shoved the old man aside and hauled her up into the boat. She was vaguely aware of flopping over the gunwale like a gaffed fish. At least, she thought, as she tried to put herself back together, this ought to convince Chris's grandad that she was just an ordinary girl.

"We better take her around to her father's boat," said the boy who held the line.

"He'll kill us," said the other.

But they were clearly alarmed at finding themselves with this unhinged old man and a girl who had nearly become his victim.

The wind felt icy as it cut through Joellen's wet clothes. She was shivering too hard to speak, but she helped herself to Chris's sleeping bag, opening it up with shaking fingers and clutching it around her.

Chris's grandad sat on the center thwart and gaped at her. She avoided his eyes, which had looked crazed in those seconds of struggle. She couldn't tell whether he had been trying to drag her on board or to push her all the way under. Maybe he hadn't known either. Whatever the impulse, it had come from somewhere so deep in his past that it linked him to Flora in a way he could never have understood.

She longed to tell him, not so that he could be rid of the ghost but so that he would know that girl with pity instead of fear. But this was for Chris to do.

Joellen could see now that Chris must have begun to figure it out when he made the connection between her storymaking and Flora's. He had recognized what was real in Joellen's imaginary island girl, and then he had guessed that this was exactly what Flora had done, finding a way to preserve what she could neither live with nor live without. Probably when the new keeper took charge and Margaret Fossett and her son Amos and the younger children had to move, they had taken Flora with them. But Flora had left her child self behind, bound to the island by grief and loss.

"You okay?" the boy in the stern asked Joellen. Then he added, "I think I've seen you before."

She nodded. It dawned on her that these were the boys who had tried to force her to change her course sailing here last weekend. She didn't want to get into that now, so she tried to say they had probably seen each other around Ledgeport, but her teeth began to chatter again. As soon as she could talk, she had more important things to deal with. Here was her chance to unload those questions she had been carrying around in her head.

"I don't guess we can set Gary out here," said the boy in the bow, "till we find out what got Chris sick."

They were scudding over the water, rounding Folly Point. Joellen caught a glimpse of sheep turning tail and taking off for the woods.

"Slow down," she said, annoyed at these boys' disregard for ducks and sheep and boats under sail, and probably anything else in their way. Then, having found her voice again, she added, "You can forget about setting anyone on this island. At least until after mid-August. And if you're coming alongside my dad's boat, you better be slow and quiet."

When neither boy responded, she forced herself to look Chris's grandad squarely in the eye. Then she asked him what his grandmother's name was.

He didn't seem to understand that she was speaking to him.

"Your grandmother's name," she said, outstaring him. "What was it?"

He had to drop his eyes before answering. "Nan. Nana."

"That was her name?"

The boy in the bow tapped the old man's shoulder to get his attention. "What did other people call her?"

"Oh. Called her Flo."

Joellen nodded. Just to make absolutely sure, she went on to ask him about Edwin and Margaret Fossett's oldest son. "And your grandfather, the one who was your nan's husband, they called him Amos?"

"Don't know. Never knew my grandfather. Never heard folks talk to him."

"But was that his name?"

"Oh, yes." He nodded. "Yes, it was."

She wasn't quite finished, and already they were zooming up to Dread Mans Cove. It was distracting to find herself so close to its gaping mouth. It seemed to suck in every waterborne thing that came near. For a time she had wrongly imagined it in Patrick Healy's account of the shipwreck. The forbidding cliff and powerful crosscurrents and ominous name, all so suggestive of drama, had misled her. It had taken Chris's practical knowledge of the cove to set her straight.

When they were safely past it, she asked her final question. "What did your grandmother look like?"

This seemed to take the old man by surprise. "Why," he said, "she looked like my nan."

The boys laughed, but Joellen pressed on. Of course Flora had been old when she raised the boy who grew into this man. Unless he had a picture, he wouldn't be able to describe her as a girl or a young woman. "Was there anything wrong with her?" Joellen said. "Did she walk all right?"

"Of course," Chris's grandad answered. "She went everywhere she needed to. Never kept her from keeping up, that foot, not even in her last years."

Joellen leaned toward him. "What was the foot like?"

His brows drew together. He started to speak, shook his head, and then showed her instead. His hands flat on the thwart became feet. The right hand turned in at an angle, the fingers crooked and raised, the heel of the palm rolled onto the base of the thumb. "Didn't trouble her none," he said. "Didn't hardly slow her."

36

Getting down from the headland turned out to be a bigger deal than Chris had suspected. He had thought Joellen's old man was out of his tree rigging him up in one of those yachting harnesses and a lifeline. The one miscalculation was that John Roth refused to wait for Joellen. He was anxious. Now that he was all packed up, he wanted to get the job done. That meant making Chris into a kind of ballast in the dinghy while it was still suspended on the slipway.

The amazing thing was that this weird system worked. The first stage on the ladder was the hardest. Even with Joellen's dad right below, even with him pressed up against Chris when things got dicey, Chris wasn't at all sure he'd make it to the dinghy.

After that it was a matter of trust. Joellen's father insisted that Chris lie flat, his legs under the thwart, the oars on either side of him. He even had to submit to being hitched to the cleats. It made his stomach turn over, not with a new attack of cramps, but with the knowledge, still fresh in his mind, of Mr. Hardison's victims roped together.

The rest of the maneuver was over in a matter of seconds, Joellen's dad easing the dinghy down and then waiting, poised for the wave that would carry them off. He left Chris hitched and confined until he had the dinghy snubbed tight to the sloop.

He stowed things in the cabin while he waited for Abbie to call to him that Joellen was back. Chris, who sat in the cockpit to stay out of the way, heard and then saw the small boat that had come around past the lighthouse. At first he didn't realize that Joellen and Grandad were sitting between Andy and Eric, Joellen wrapped in his sleeping bag. What had she gone and got herself into?

He started to stand up to wave, but he was too unsteady to risk crumpling ingloriously in front of that audience. Instead he leaned down the companionway and told Joellen's father what was happening.

Despite all the confusion, it didn't take long to work out the few details about returning to Ledgeport. Andy and Eric couldn't understand why Chris wouldn't just hop in the boat and come home as they'd planned. Joellen's dad told them it was out of the question. Then he had to reassure the grandad about Chris's condition. Even so, he still wasn't about to let Chris go back in an open boat.

Joellen didn't hang around to hear all of this play out. She went below to get into dry clothes. By the time she was back in the cockpit, the boat with Andy, Eric, and Chris's grandad was speeding off, and Dad was frowning at its wake, which made the dinghy grind against *Dovekie*.

After he rowed ashore to get Abbie, Joellen sat across from Chris and waited for him to say something. If he asked her how she had landed in the drink, she would simply say that she had slipped. He didn't need to know more, at least not now. Anyway, it would be awhile before she could try to figure out what had happened. Or almost happened.

Chris shoved one hand into a pocket and held it there. Finally he spoke. "How was Grandad when he saw you there instead of me?"

"Ballistic," she replied. "Like you predicted. How was Dad while I was gone?"

"Not that bad."

She grinned at him. "I got some answers out of your grandad. It was hard not to tell him what they were about. Did you make sure my knapsack's aboard?" She had stuffed everything into it, notebook, journal, printouts, and all the pieces of oilskin wrapping.

"Abbie took it with the other stuff. Your dad probably stowed it. And there's something else we didn't leave behind." Withdrawing his hand from his pocket, he held out the bracelet, Flora's keepsake.

Joellen said, "Oh." That was all.

He said, "Don't you want it?"

She did. She wanted it so much that she was almost afraid to take it from him.

It seemed to him absolutely right that she have it. The bracelet was hers because she had searched and searched for it and also because she had come so close to Flora. Reaching forward to hand it to her, he had to grab the bulkhead cleat to keep from pitching forward. "What do you suppose it'll look like when it's cleaned up?" he said.

Joellen shook her head. "It's—" She had to search for words. "It's real." And then: "It's what I imagined."

She knew if she put it on her wrist, it would be even harder to give it up. But she had to think of what Flora would have done if the bracelet had been recovered in her time. "Anyhow," she continued, "it wasn't much when Flora had it. But it was a gift from her father." She got up and put it back in his hand. "So it belongs to your grandad now. Think what it will mean for him to have one great-grandfather's honor back and another great-grandfather's token from a peat bog."

Chris shoved the bracelet into his pocket again. He was suddenly, mightily exhausted. Joellen's dad had made it clear that he was to stay in the cabin out of the wind during the homeward sail. He wished he were below already. He wanted to lie under a blanket, away from the dazzling light. He considered climbing down but couldn't figure out how to make his body manage the steps. He decided to wait for Joellen's dad to help.

The dinghy was coming now. In a few minutes they would be under way.

Joellen looked up at the headland. From down here only the top of the lighthouse was visible. But on the cliffs facing the mooring every burrow opening stood out like so many dark, unblinking eyes watching the intruders prepare to give the island back to itself.

On one of the highest shelves of turf a puffin squeezed out from a burrow, cocked its head, stretched in the sun, and flapped its stumpy wings. A shadow passed over it. Instantly the puffin dived back inside the cliff. Glancing skyward, Joellen caught a glimpse of the shadow maker, a great black-backed gull cruising over its hunting grounds.

That's how it had always been. Joellen knew that. The shadow would return tomorrow and the next day, whenever the sun shone, and again on the precarious moonlit night in August, when that puffin's chick stepped boldly out of the underground darkness to tumble into the sea.

Light and shadow, both. That's how it was.

HISTORICAL
NOTE

The Irish famine of 1846–49 resulted from a fungal blight that destroyed the potato crops, almost the sole food available to the Irish, and from an economic policy that prohibited the Irish from consuming all other produce, which was controlled by British landholders and raised for export.

Because of the oppressive British rule, most of the Irish who sought passage to North America wanted to avoid British Canada. But states like New York and Massachusetts passed statutes designed to keep out the destitute famine survivors, and the journey to New York or Boston cost more than three times the passage to New Brunswick and Quebec.

Those who could afford to go to the United States and were well enough to gain entry very often ended up in the clutches of men, known as runners, who went aboard the ships from Ireland, offered help and guidance, and succeeded in robbing or simply exploiting the weary and confused passengers.

In Ireland speculators continued to cram desperate emigrants into overcrowded ships without sanitary facilities or the legal quotas of water and food. Passengers arrived in North America screaming for water. In 1847, 109,000 people left for Canada. Officials set up quarantine stations, the most infamous on Grosse Isle in the St. Lawrence. Passengers still healthy on arrival tended to become sick in quarantine or while waiting to disembark into the quarantine sheds.

The line of ships waiting to unload passengers was sometimes several miles long. But the sick and helpless kept on coming. Landlords sent them as an alternative to eviction, since the cost of shipping one person (under those appalling conditions) was less than keeping him or her in a workhouse for a year. Lord Palmerston's tenants, for instance, reached St. John in November "almost in a state of nudity." The citizens of St. John offered them free passage and food if they would agree to return to Ireland. Yet, for Lord Palmerston's Irish estates, this emigration policy was a success.

Sometimes, because of overcrowding in the fever sheds, quarantine was maintained on board the waiting ships. One such ship, arriving with 427 passengers, had only 150 alive after fifteen days of quarantine. It is estimated that in one year, 1847, 17,000 Irish died at sea and 20,000 on arrival in Canada.

Despite the fact that the captains of U.S. ferryboats at St. John and on Lake Champlain refused passage to the Irish, many did succeed in crossing the border. Irish communities grew up in some small Maine towns. One of Eastport's oldest inhabitants, interviewed a few years ago, retained some of the Irish phrasing passed on to him by those in his family who walked down from St. John and settled in a part of Eastport, Maine, first known as Irish Hollow.

These survivors were among the fortunate. An inscription on a monument commemorating those who died and were buried in mass graves on Grosse Isle states:

IN THIS SECLUDED SPOT LIE THE MORTAL REMAINS
OF 5,294 PERSONS, WHO, FLYING FROM PESTILENCE
AND FAMINE IN IRELAND IN THE YEAR 1847,
FOUND IN AMERICA BUT A GRAVE.